I0746044

River Bend

Julie Kay

River Bend

Thank you from the heart...

To my wonderful group of first readers, who have always supported me so positively, Sharon, Wendy and Deb.

To my incredibly talented niece who guided me through the process of publishing as well as, designing my cover. I love it Molly!

For the loyalty and support of my biggest fan, my sister Sharon. I could definitely not do this writing gig without you. You read every draft and story I have ever written, always improving my words.

And of course, to those I love the most, Jon, Annie, Nick, Kirsty and Harper.

1

Chapter One

The small blue Nissan Pulsar took off carefully from the curb joining the steady stream of work traffic. Behind the wheel, Lara Benton took a deep breath and exhaled slowly. *This is it,* she thought merging onto the freeway heading towards her new future. *River Bend here I come.* As she got into the motion of city driving, she thought about the decision that had got her to this very moment in her life. She had been about to start university when the pandemic hit and annoyingly had to complete her degree online. Not only did that damn pandemic ruin her dream of physically going to uni and all that goes with that, it also put a major wedge in her romantic life. Well, more like a knife than a wedge. Lara shuddered just thinking about what her life had been like at that time. *Yeah, done and dusted just like her and Josh.* This was her new beginning.

Lara reached over to adjust the air conditioning. It was already hitting the low 20's and it was only 8am. It was going to be a scorcher of a day. The reporter on the radio had just finished saying that the temperature was going to be in the high thirties. Lara pulled up at a set of lights, she mentally checked her schedule. Lunch around one and then only another three hours to get to her motel, stay the night and get up early to be at her destination before lunch time.

The little Pulsar pulled out of the city and hit the Bolte Bridge, Lara had the whole view of Melbourne in her sights. It certainly wasn't the prettiest view but it always made Lara feel like the city meets the country. Like she was leaving the city behind for greener pastures. She pressed the button to lower her window and took in a large breath of the city air. *Well, it would be a while before she breathed in that air again, from here on it would be fresh country air for her.* The little car found its groove and took off with all the other commuters or holiday makers travelling up the Hume towards her new home. On the side of the road the houses started to thin out and tall eucalypts trees dotted the verge, their white bark contrasting with the blue of the sky. From one of the tall trees a flock of noisy white feathers exploded into the sky and spread out like lazy clouds. The cockatoos, with their dots of yellow crowns, seemed to follow her for a few minutes and then banked left to take off across the fields as if they had been summoned by the wind. The road went on inching Lara toward her destination. She reached over and fiddled with the controls of the radio as she started to lose contact with the latest pop song.

Pulling over at a servo she emerged from the car to stretch her tired legs. *Macca's will get me through the next few hours,* she thought, as she walked through the glass sliding doors and ordered a cheeseburger, fries and a double strength cappuccino to go.

Once back in the car Lara headed towards her new destination. She had applied for the job right after she had returned from her travels in Europe. She had put her whole life on hold during the pandemic and now she was not going to be held back. Working and living in Melbourne was not an option for her any more. She physically shook her head and straightened her shoulders, *don't go down that rabbit hole Lara,* she thought.

She'd taken a whirlwind trip to Europe after the ban on overseas travel was lifted. She remembered the sparkling blue waters of the Greek island of Santorini, the white stone buildings reflecting like shimmering stars against the bright blue sky and water. If she concentrated hard enough, she could almost smell the chargrilled calamari being cooked over open fires on the black volcanic beaches, the salty smell mingling with sun lotion and freedom. Yes freedom. Freedom to truly be herself and not someone's idea of who she should be. Yes, the lockdown definitely did her no favours but then she wasn't the only one carrying baggage, even if she thought hers was too heavy to bear at times. This new chapter in her life was exactly that, a brand-new chapter with none of the old stuff. But Lara knew that she had to be strong enough to bury it all deep down while she started her new life as the young, confident, professional school teacher.

Using the GPS on her phone she found the cheap motel that she had booked online in Melbourne. The row of grey coloured doors were not welcoming at all but the lady at reception seemed friendly enough. Her room comprised of two side tables, two single beds with plain brown bedspreads, a desk and a small checkered ensuite. *Cheap but definitely not cheerful.* Lara unpacked her overnight bag and walked to the only food establishment in the small town, the local pub. After a bowl of Thai chicken curry and a glass of white wine she made her way back to her small room and got out her laptop. Her boss at River Bend Primary School had already sent her a list of her students. Lara went through her work program again for week one, googling different 'getting to know you' activities. The realisation that she was going to be an actual teacher sent thrills coursing through her body.

River Bend was about as remote a place you could be in country Victoria. It was on the border of New South Wales and South Australia, probably closer to Adelaide than Melbourne looking at the map. The countryside changed from green to red and then back to green depending on how close you were to the Murray River. When she was a small child, her parents had taken her to Echuca to ride on the Emmylou paddle steamer. She remembered going into the captain's lookout and having a photo taken, the captain's hat on her head and her small hands on the steering wheel as if she were in charge of the whole boat. Beautiful green willow trees seemed to dance at the side of the big brown river.

The next morning Lara got up early and went to the motel dining room where she had a simple breakfast of cereal and toast. She was excited to be finally reaching her new home today. After an hour of driving, she passed a sign that read, 'River Bend 70 Kilometres.' The forest on the side of the road was thick with vegetation. The tall eucalyptus trees were so close together that it was hard at times to tell which branch belonged to which tree. Shadows danced against the dark brown bark giving the forest a secretive, almost sinister appearance. In parts there were felled trees as if some type of machine had gone through culling parts of the tall strong countryside to let in the light. The noisy miners annoyed a flock of rosellas and caused them to lift to the sky in a flash of red and green, their mournful screeches reached Lara through the closed windows of her car. And then like an oasis through the tangled branches, the blue glistening of a large reservoir sparkled in the bright sunlight and refreshed the scene in front of her. The dark forest was forgotten as the lake reflected off the surrounding green hills. The next sign read, River Bend population 2,800. Lara smiled and thought, 2,801.

2

Chapter Two

The main street looked deserted in the harsh heat of the afternoon sun. The verandas on either side of the road gave off limited shade. Lara drove past the brittle medium strip with pale yellow daisies poking through the cracking, hard soil. As she drove past the clock tower a brown flash jumped out in front of her hitting the bonnet. The thud echoed throughout the car. Pushing her foot down as hard as she could on the brake, the car stayed still as Lara's body kept moving forward hitting her head on the exploding airbag, projecting her head right back to the headrest and then pushing her body forward again.

'Oh. My. God what was that?' Lara said. She touched her hand to her forehead and felt the sticky wetness of her own blood on her fingertips.

'Miss, Miss are you okay?' A tall man knocked his knuckles on her car window.

'What the hell was that?' Lara said, fumbling with the door latch trying to get the door open around the bulk of the air bag.

'It was a bloody roo, it jumped right in front of you,' said a deep male voice. 'Here come over to the shade and I'll take a look at your head.' He bent down gently clasping her arm and helped Lara manoeuvre herself around the airbag and out of the car.

'Hey Marg, can you go to the station and grab the first aid kit and tell Sarge what's happened?' continued the young man, who Lara now realised was in a light blue, short-sleeve police shirt and shorts. Two older grey-haired ladies stood behind him.

'Oh no, I don't feel so good. I think I'm seeing double,' Lara said to the policeman who guided her onto the sidewalk.

'What... oh no,' he chuckled, looking behind him, 'that's the Early twins, they're identical. You just think you're seeing double.'

The Early twins nodded their heads in unison looking on in bewildered silence at the drama unfolding in front of them.

'Here, sit down and I'll take a look at that cut. It looks kind of nasty.' He took a fresh handkerchief from his pocket.

Who carries handkerchiefs nowadays with the invention of tissues, thought Lara, as he placed his hand over the hanky to stem the flow of blood. He was leaning over her and Lara could see his dark chest hairs peeking out from the v of his shirt, a whiff of woody pine hit her nose. She hadn't been this close to a man since Josh and feelings she thought were deep buried started to tingle down her spine. *Not the time or place Lara.*

'I'll go get water,' said one of the Early twins, pushing through the nearest door. From where Lara sat it looked like a kind of local hall.

'Bring her inside the hall Curtis, it's a lot cooler,' the other grey-haired lady said, motioning them all towards the door.

Lara got up slowly from the bench seat she had been balancing on and followed the twin into the hall with Curtis gently placing his hand on her arm for support. When she was settled on a black plastic chair he left to go and inspect the damaged car.

When the cool air hit her, Lara started to feel a bit wobbly.

'Oh no pet, stay there and I'll go and put on the kettle. A nice strong sweet cup of tea is exactly what's needed here. There is no problem that a good cup of tea can't fix.' One of the twins took off through a back door just as the other one sat next to Lara and opened up a medical kit.

'I just don't know what happened to Marg. She was meant to go and get help, I'm Shirl by the way and my sister's name is Pearl,' tusked the twin.

'Sorry to be such a bother, Shirl. Honestly, I'm feeling much better now. Not so wobbly.'

'Oh no love I'm not having a go at you; it's Marg, she's been so sad lately... Anyway pet, not your circus, not your monkey,' she said, and patted Lara kindly on the knee. 'Now I think the bleeding has stopped, so that's one good thing at least.'

'Here you go pet,' the other twin returned with a tray of assorted cups and a big red and white spotted teapot.

Just then the front door opened and the lady from the accident, presumably Marg, and an older man came in carrying a black doctor's bag. 'Here she is Smithy, the poor girl just driving through our town and this happens to her,' said the lady, pointing towards Lara as she sipped her sweet tea with shaky hands.

Lara looked up at the doctor and couldn't help admiring his kind blue eyes and smiling demeanor. 'I am so sorry for the fuss. Honestly you didn't have to bring a doctor. The blood has stopped and I'm feeling way better. Thanks for the tea, ah Shirley,' said Lara.

'Oh no love, I'm Pearl not Shirl,' laughed the twin.

'Yes dear don't get too confused, you have a one in two chance of getting their names correct and I've been here forty years and I still can't tell them apart,' laughed the doctor. 'I'm Doc Smith but everyone calls me Smithy and that's Marg,' he said, nodding towards the other lady. 'Now let's have a look. I reckon a couple of steri-strips will do the job just nicely.' Smithy bent over her and cleaned the blood away with a cotton ball and then applied the strips. 'I will prescribe a couple of Panadol and you should be as right as rain dear. Not reindeer,' he laughed, 'right as rain, no deer.'

Lara looked back and forth at the four faces staring at her, and felt a warmth and safety envelop her. Whether it was from the shock or the bump on her head or just their kindness, tears started to well in her eyes.

'Oh sweetheart it's not the end of the world, no one was seriously injured, well maybe the kangaroo,' said Pearl or Shirl. Just then the door opened and Curtis came in.

'How's my poor car?' Lara looked up at Curtis and quickly flicked the tears away with her fingers.

'I've contacted our local mechanic and he reckons he can have it fixed in a couple of days. Where were you headed?' He picked up the big pot and sloshed himself a cup of tea. Lara couldn't help staring at his biceps. In fact, now that she was feeling more like her old self, she just couldn't stop staring at everything about Mr. Curtis the policeman.

'Ah, I'm actually going to be living here in River Bend. I'm the new primary school teacher, Lara Benton.'

'Did you hear that Curtis, Lara must be the one that's boarding with your Janie? Lovely to meet you Lara, just bad luck it's under these circumstances,' said Marg with a smile.

I knew it was too good to be true. He's clearly taken, thought Lara with a small huff.

Everyone nodded and crowded around Lara, smiling now that they knew she was going to become part of their community.

'So the new primary school teacher hey. You'll have to deal with my young grandson Eli. You couldn't pay me enough.' Smithy laughed and grabbed a Scotch Finger from the tray, dunking it in his tea.

'Hey now Smithy, that's a bit over the top. Let's not scare off our newest addition to River Bend so soon, she's already had a terrible start, poor love,' scoffed Marg, as she refilled cups of tea and then passed around the tray of Arnott's Biscuits.

'Well Lara, you stay here and rest and I'll go and see to your car and luggage. I've rung the council to come and take the kangaroo away,' said Curtis, putting down his cup and getting ready to leave.

'Oh no, I think it's just hit me that I've killed a living thing,' Lara said in horror. 'I feel terrible.'

The twin that seemed slightly smaller, maybe Pearl stood up with her hands on her hips and said 'Don't be silly, the stupid thing should know better than to come into town and cause havoc. It got into old mate Jenison's garden and trampled the roses. He will be fit to be tied when he comes out of the Rivy Arms.'

'Okay then Lara come with us and we'll take you to Janie's while young Curtis deals with the road kill and smashed car,' said Smithy, getting up from his chair and moving towards the door.

The little party poured out of the hall. They turned right and walked two doors up to what looked like a local cafe. They all piled in beckoning Lara to join them.

'No, I really don't feel like having another cuppa. I think I need to just meet Janie and get settled in,' replied Lara, turning around ready to head back out into the street and find the good-looking policeman.

'Oh, silly this is where you will be living if you are boarding with Janie,' said the smaller twin, beckoning Lara into the establishment.

Behind the counter of the 'Cozy, Cup & Wares' stood the most gorgeous girl Lara had seen in a long time. Her dark curly hair was casually pulled up into a top knot with a wisp of curls cascading around her face. She was tall and slim and was dressed in a gingham maxi skirt with a white t-shirt French tucked. Lara had always wanted to pull off that look but always felt self-conscious when she tried it and ended up having to re-iron her shirt.

'Well, what's going on here then? Is there a fire I don't know about?' said the girl behind the counter in a singsong voice.

Of course, this would have to be Janie, the cute cop's girlfriend.

'Janie we have just rescued your new house mate Lara from a small car accident. Lara, meet Janie, our own entrepreneur,' Smithy said, sweeping his hand over the shop. It was really quite beautiful with homewares, jewellery, books, mismatched tables and chairs dotted around, and a beautiful red brick fireplace and couch at the side of the large room. At closer inspection there even seemed to be a courtyard with plants and tables out the back.

'God Lara, not the nicest welcome to River Bend a girl could hope for. Look at your poor head, it looks so sore,' said Janie, coming around from the counter and pulling Lara into a tight bear hug. She smelt of cinnamon and fresh coffee beans.

'Lovely to meet you Janie, and honestly it probably looks worse than it is. I'm actually pretty lucky. Everyone's been so kind, especially your boyfriend Curtis.'

'Boyfriend!' laughed Janie. Just as she was about to say something else the door opened and in came Curtis carrying bags and boxes. He placed them down in the corner of the cafe and stood up looking at all the faces staring at him.

'So, here's your *boyfriend,*' said Smithy, doing air quotes with his fingers.

'Oh, ignore them Lara, Curtis is my little brother NOT my boyfriend. I just shudder to think,' she laughed.

With everyone staring at her and laughing, Lara felt her cheeks go crimson, whether it was the knock on the head or her heightened emotions she really wished the floor would open up and swallow her.

'Listen, thanks everyone. If you could just show me where I'm staying Janie, I'll get out of everyone's hair.'

Lara's Research:

Not your circus, not your monkey: Don't drag me into your drama—I'm not getting involved.

Fit to be tied: extreme anger or agitation.

3

Chapter Three

Janie shooed everyone out of the cafe and put the 'closed' sign on the door.

'They're a bit much but their hearts are in the right place. Now you've had a fright so I'll take you upstairs and show you the apartment. Hopefully you like it. I used to run it as an Airbnb before the school asked me to let it to you full time. I've asked Curtis to take your stuff up the front stairs.'

Lara followed Janie out through the lovely back courtyard, stepping around the velvet couches and Mediterranean tiled tables and chairs heading towards a flight of beautifully carved stairs.

'There's a side entrance through that gate over there that goes up to the front veranda, I'll show you later. You actually don't even have to step foot inside the cafe if you don't want to.'

Together they walked up the stairs and Janie got an old fashion key out of her pocket and opened an ornate wooden door at the top of the landing.

'Fingers crossed you like it,' she said, stepping aside to let Lara get the full view.

It was stunning. There was a small entrance way with a side table big enough for keys and a handbag. The space opened into a beautiful sun filled bedroom with a small kitchenette off to the side. The double bed had a white vintage bedspread with coloured throw rugs draped every-where and a carved antique camphor wood chest at the end. There was a rust camelback sofa on the wall next to the bed with a small walnut coffee table in front. Above the couch the wall was adorned with black and white pictures that looked to be of the surrounding area in eclectic frames. The small kitchenette had a two burner, stainless steel stove top and a stainless-steel oven, kettle and microwave. The cabinets were made from the same walnut as the coffee table. Big French doors opened onto a wooden balcony that hugged the front of the building. Lara could see a white wrought iron outdoor setting through the glass. Thick, rust coloured velvet drapes hung at the side of each door. Next to the kitchen there was a doorway that led to a small ensuite. It was simply stunning. Lara couldn't believe her luck to get such a comfortable and stylish place for her very own. She felt like pinching herself, she was so happy.

'Curtis put your luggage out on the balcony before he went back to work. I'll give you a hand bringing it in and then maybe get a bit settled and come down for dinner around six if you feel like company. We live in the cottage out the back.' Janie dragged Lara's brown suitcase from the balcony and pushed it next to the bed.

'Thanks so much Janie, I appreciate it. This place is absolutely stunning and I love it.' Lara turned and gave Janie one of her best and brightest smiles. 'I'll see you at six. Is there anything you want me to bring, alcohol, cake? Is there a bottle shop or something around here?'

'There is but honestly please just bring yourself. It's the least we can do after your terrible introduction to River Bend.' At that she waved goodbye and gently closed the door leaving Lara on her own to settle in.

After a soothing hot shower Lara dressed in a yellow off the shoulder maxi dress that accentuated her small slim figure and full breasts. Her bright blue eyes shone in the bathroom light. With her long dark brown hair tied up in a high ponytail, she grabbed the box of Cadbury chocolates that her friend had given her as a going away gift. There was no way she would ever go to someone's house without some type of thank-you gift, her mother would never forgive her.

When she arrived at the cottage behind the café Janie and Curtis were sitting outside on a small wrought iron table enjoying a glass of wine. Janie had made a scrumptious vegetarian lasagne with a home-grown tomato salad. Everything about Janie's house was eclectic. Miss-matched furniture and dinner ware, candles and fairy lights adorned the garden with the smell of roses wafting around. This was the country garden of Lara's dreams. Climbing red roses adorned the wire trellises between the cottage and the cafe. There was a country garden with petals of pink, purple and red everywhere along the side of the fence. Busy bees flew in and out of the colourful flowers drinking the sweet nectar. There was even a very productive veggie patch at the front of the house with a healthy looking show of beans, tomatoes and pumpkins.

Curtis filled her glass with a local pinot noir and the three fell into easy conversation.

Janie sipped her red contentedly and asked, 'So Lara, what made you decide to come to the country for your first job?'

'I suppose all the stuff we went through during the lockdown in the city. I just needed to get out and see a bit of the world rather than stay at home with Mum and Dad. I did the big Contiki trip at the beginning of the year, once we were allowed to travel. You know, seeing ten countries in three months. When I got back, I did CRT work in different schools in my area.'

'CRT?' interrupted Curtis, with a raised eyebrow.

'Casual relief teaching, great money but tricky because you never know what grade you will get. But anyway, it was amazing so I kind of feel like I can now settle down for a bit and really get my teeth into teaching and see what I think. I loved my placements and CRT jobs, so I think I'm really going to love teaching here. I just can't wait to get my own grade, set up my room, and meet the kids.'

'Yeah, I'm hearing you Lara, it was a shitty time but now we have to move on and it sounds like you have it all sorted,' said Curtis, reaching for a Cadbury Favourite, unwrapping it and popping it in his mouth.

'Were you a police man here in River Bend during Covid Curtis?' Lara asked.

'Yeah, at that time my boss was Sergeant Perry and he was pretty relaxed about it all. I mean as far as the locals go but not the out of towners that came through. I reckon we gave out heaps of fines but we were lenient on the locals. Perry passed away at the end of 2022 and now I have a new boss. Senior Sergeant Barrington is a very different version to old Perry, that's for sure,' he said, shaking his head sadly as he remembered his old boss.

'I'm sorry to hear about your boss Curtis. It must have been a shock. It wasn't Covid related, was it?' Lara asked quietly.

'Nah nothing like that, anyway it was a while ago now but I still miss him,' he replied sadly, his green eyes misting over as if he was remembering some distant time.

'To change the subject Curtis, what's happening with this mysterious snowdropper that's hanging around the town?' mentioned Janie, as she also popped a Favourite in her mouth.

'Snowdropper, please explain?' Lara laughed.

'What you haven't heard of that term, Lara? It's someone that sneaks around stealing women's undies and bras. Disgusting. It must be a country slang word,' explained Janie.

'Well, we haven't had anybody reporting anything since the Early twins last month,' replied Curtis.

'Seriously, the Early twins... That's just wrong on so many levels,' laughed Lara. 'Oh, I shouldn't be so rude but I'm just thinking about what their smalls would look like and I'm not picturing satin and lace.'

'So satin and lace hey Lara,' winked Curtis, raising his eyebrows just slightly. She noticed how his green eyes crinkled up at the corners, giving him a roguish look when he laughed. *How could anyone be this cute?* she thought.

'Stop it Curtis,' said Lara, giving him a swat on the arm. 'I mean, how do *you* imagine the Early Twins lingerie?'

'I don't have to imagine it, they brought in a matching pair for us to photograph. But seriously this is happening more and more to random women, at different places and different ages so it's becoming quite a problem in the town. My advice to you ladies is dry your smalls inside.'

'Maybe we could set up a trap. You know, put some really sexy stuff out and get one of those security cameras from Bunnings in Talbot and catch the snowdropper red handed. Barrington would be so impressed you'd get a promotion and be the local hero,' laughed Janie, as she grabbed some of the dirty dishes to take inside.

'Here let me help. That's a great idea, Janie. Curtis, I can just see the headlines...' said Lara, reaching over and piling up the dinner plates. 'Cozy, Cup & Wares catches panty thief using own undies.'

'Snowdropper of River Bend, caught by young, good looking, and very single Constable Gold,' said Janie, pointing out the words in the night sky.

'Okay, okay you two, very funny. But as I said, just mind your own undies instead of worrying about everyone else's,' he laughed.

4

Chapter Four

The next morning Lara went for a walk around the town to get the lay of the land. She moseyed on past the IGA where she realised she could get her groceries and alcohol, as well as, Tattslotto. Next door to the IGA was the 'Cut & Shine' a women and men's hairdressing salon, and then next to that was what looked like a small hardware and feed store, the sign above the door read 'Olsen Brothers'. On the corner was the Riverdale Arms, it was a majestic old building with leadlight windows and a wrap-around balcony with wrought iron banisters. It looked like it was one of the town's original buildings. Down the side there was a beer garden with brightly coloured umbrellas and wooden tables dotted around, and presiding over the whole area was the most magnificent silver birch tree Lara had ever seen. It's peeling white and brown bark contrasted with the bright green of the tree's teardrop shaped leaves. On the side of the old sandstone building was a hanging bougainvillea of a deep purple. *What a lovely place to have a cold wine on a hot day,* she thought. Over the road from the pub was the police station which was also built in old sandstone, *well that's convenient for the pub* thought Lara and wondered if sexy policeman Curtis was in the building. Next to the police station was what looked like an op shop, then a clothing emporium and the Country Woman's Association Hall that she had been in the day before, the Cozy, Cup & Wares with her place up the top, and a mechanics with a small petrol bowser out the front. The median strip in the middle of the road was being mowed by council workers and there were bits of brown grass flying everywhere. There was a strip of colourful flowers being watered by another worker who looked determined that this little parcel of Australia was going to have some colour in it no matter the cost of the water he was using. She was glad to see that there was no evidence left that an animal had been hit and killed the day before. It really was one of the prettiest towns Lara had seen in country Victoria. She stepped onto the street avoiding the busy council workers who gave her a customary nod, and crossed over to see if the mechanic was in.

'Hello, anyone here?' called out Lara into the dark of the shed. She could see a row of black tyres on one side of the repair shop, and a hoist with a red ute dangling from it. The building smelt of oil, petrol and month-old dust. She could see her Pulsar at the back of the building almost hiding amongst the dust motes.

A man came out from a side door wiping his hands on an old cloth. 'Hello you must be the owner,' he said, pointing to her car.

'Yes, I'm afraid she's mine. What's the damage? I didn't really get a good look at it yesterday; I was whisked away by half the town,' Lara laughed.

'It's really only a fender bender. Once I fix the bumper, she should be good to go. However, it may take a bit more time to get the new airbags sorted, but I've been onto Nissan and ordered them. I can probably have it ready for you later in the week if that works,' he said, handing her the quote on an A4 sized paper.

'Oh thanks. I'm Lara by the way, I'm the new primary school teacher.'

'Nice to meet you Lara, I'm Bob Duncan and it seems you will be teaching my Toby. He told me he was getting a new teacher. I'll be able to go home and tell him I've met you first,' he laughed.

'Well great, thanks Bob, here's my mobile number. Just give me a call when the car is ready. Oh, and tell Toby I said hello.' Lara headed out of town towards the river with the sound of the kookaburras laughing in the distance. The picnic area was pretty deserted this time of day but there was an old black ute with a caravan that looked like it had come out of the dark ages. No sleek curves of silver and steal, just white with a dirty brown strip around the middle. There was a blonde-haired lady sitting on a deck chair reading and two small children playing on a colourful mat. 'Hi,' waved Lara, as she headed down towards the dry riverbed. The two small girls jumped up and raced after her dragging a blue beach cart filled with sand toys behind them.

'Don't go far girls,' said the mother, before putting her nose back in her book.

'Hello, what's your name?' asked one of the little girls.

'Oh hi. I'm Lara,' she said, realising her quiet walk was going to be interrupted by these two chatterboxes.

'I'm Elsie and that's Harper. She doesn't talk much but I do so if you need to know anything let me know not her. So, what are you doing? We are going to build a sandcastle down on the riverbed. Do you want to help?' said Elsie, without taking a single breath.

'Oh, I think I'll let you two work on the castle and then on my way back I'll come and inspect it and give you a score out of ten. How does that sound?'

'Awesome come on Harps, we have a castle to build.' The two little girls headed off in the other direction and stopped when they hit the soft red sand of the dry riverbank. Lara continued on, noticing that drought had hit this part of the world severely. What was probably once a fast-flowing river was now cracked hard mud and tufts of spinifex grass. The tall ghost gums stood majestically along the bank having sucked their last bit of water from the flow months ago. Luckily the Australian eucalyptus trees don't need watering like many other trees do and thrive in the harsh Aussie bush environment. As the noon sun hit their green foliage Lara turned back, starting to get anxious that little Elsie and Harper would be waiting for her to critique their castle. When she rounded the bend she was relieved to see that the shade of one of the gums was directly over them. Lara shook her head judging their mother for not keeping a better eye on the small girls.

'Hey Lara, we've just finished. Come over here and take a look,' waved Elsie, beckoning for Lara to walk over.

'Wow girls this is amazing. I particularly like the way you have put the gum leaves and twigs in for decoration. Definitely a ten out of ten.' The two girls clapped their hands together in joy.

In the distance Lara could hear the girl's mum calling for them. It must be lunch time. Lara followed the girls up the winding bank and back to their caravan.

'Hi there, I'm Tiffany,' said the girl's mum, waving to Lara. 'Would you like to stay for lunch? We're having ham sandwiches.'

'Oh no, thanks so much, that's very kind of you but I have to get back. I have lots of unpacking to do.'

'So, you are new to River Bend just like us. My husband Brad is working as a farmhand on one of the big wheat stations out of town. Rather than stay at home alone in Melbourne, we decided to follow him out here and see what we think of it,' said Tiffany, ushering the girls to go inside and wash their hands. Lara felt a bit guilty about her earlier judgment of the mum. She seemed really nice and caring.

'The girls are excited because they will be starting at the local primary school next week.'

'Oh, well I'm Lara Benton, I'll probably be one of their teachers judging by the look of them.'

'Our teacher, yay that's so exciting,' sang Elsie, as she came out of the caravan followed by Harper.

'Lovely to meet you. Girls, say hello to Miss Benton. I'm assuming it's Miss,' she said, with an apologetic smile.

'Yes Miss Benton, hi again. We are going to have the best time girls, I'm very excited about teaching at your new school. And now that I think about it, I remember making an Elsie name tag and placemat.'

'Oh yes, yes, yes,' screamed little Elsie in excitement, clapping her tiny hands together.

After chatting with the family for a while, Lara headed back into town stopping at the IGA to pick up a few staples and something for lunch.

'Hello ahh Pearl, or is it Shirl?' asked Lara, trying not to seem rude.

'Come on it's Pearl love. Fair suck of the sav,' she laughed, throwing up her hands as if Lara should have been able to pick who was standing at the counter. 'How's that head of yours, pet? What a dog's breakfast that was yesterday. The cut looks so much better. Have you settled in?'

'Yes I have, it's a beautiful little town. I'm just going to grab a few things.' Lara picked up a basket and headed into the bowels of the shop.

'Yeah, have a Captain Cook around the place and see what you want,' called Pearl from the counter.

With her milk and tea bags she added a small loaf of bread, margarine and cheese. She didn't need anything for dinner as Janie had given her a leftover slice of lasagne and some green salad. She really wanted to buy a bottle of the pinot noir she had had at Janie's but had to settle for a different brand since the selection was not very extensive.

'Okay love that'll be $25. Will that be cash or card?' asked Pearl, putting her items into the floral carry bag Lara had pulled out of her backpack.

'Here, I'll just tap thanks Pearl.'

'Paying with cash nowadays is like writing a letter, instead, we are tapping and posting on Facebook,' she said, shaking her head and handing the bag over to Lara, smiling sweetly.

This woman really loves a saying, thought Lara as she waved goodbye and headed over the road to the Cozy, Cup & Wares.

Lara's Research:

Fair suck of the sav: an attitude of unbelief, awe, wonder or even exasperation or frustration.

Dog's breakfast: something messy or disorderly.

Captain Cook: have a look.

5

Chapter Five

Lara unwrapped the plate of lasagne and put it in the microwave and pressed five minutes. She reached over and poured another glass of wine taking it over to the small table outside on her balcony. She had a bird's eye view of the street from up here and as she went to turn around her eye caught the outline of a man standing behind one of the golden wattle trees outside of the IGA. *That's strange, he seems to be staring up at me,* she thought pursing her lips together tightly, creating a tiny, tense pout. She couldn't make out his face as he was in a dark hoodie with the hood pulled right down and sunglasses on. That was strange since it was a warm January evening. When he noticed that she had noticed him he lifted his hand to wave and turned around and walked off down the alleyway beside the IGA. *Creepy man,* she thought as a shiver went down her spine.

That night Lara watched the movie 'Love Actually' for about the tenth time. It was by far her favourite love story. For some reason her thoughts went to Goldie as she had named Curtis Gold in her mind. He was certainly a handsome man, the broadness of his shoulders left her shuddering and, oh my, how his body tapered into a trim waist, what she wouldn't give to wrap her arms around him, savouring the taste of his lips on hers. *Come on Lara get over yourself, you are sounding like a love struck teenager and you don't even know him. A bloody cop as well...He's probably a creep. No, he's definitely not a creep.* She had sworn off all men after her debacle with Josh. There was a small fling in Greece but that was all it was, a fling. She definitely wasn't interested in a serious relationship at the moment. She only cared about her career and enjoying her early twenties as an independent woman, on a new adventure in a new place. Her mind wandered to the guy that had been standing outside her balcony staring up at her. *Now that was a creep!* Just then she thought she heard a noise coming from outside her balcony door. The tone of the light behind the curtain changed as if it was being blocked by something. She went over and pulled the curtain across just as one of her pot plants fell over and she was convinced that she could hear someone running down the stairs. She bolted for the back stairs running down to the Gold's cottage and banging on the door. A sleepy Curtis wearing only a pair of denim shorts opened the door. He was raking his hand through his hair looking confused. His dark curls were practically standing on end. She noticed that his shorts were not quite done up and a patch of dark hair was visible above the waistline. *Oh. My. God he's bloody gorgeous,* she thought as her eyes moved up to his sleep tossed hair.

Curtis frowned, 'Lara, what's wrong?'

'Oh God there was someone outside my balcony door. I think they were looking at me through the slit in the curtains,' she said, as her mind clicked back into gear and she remembered how terrified she had been.

'Wait here I'll go take a look,' he said, moving past her quickly as Janie came out of the bathroom towel drying her hair.

'Gosh Lara what's wrong? Come in you poor thing you're shaking.'

Janie ushered Lara into the kitchen and put the kettle on.

'There was someone outside my balcony window. It was so scary, Janie.'

'Oh no Lara, that's terrible you must have got such a shock. Do you want a cuppa or something stronger? I'm sure Curtis will sort it all out for you.'

'Yeah, a cuppa will be fine. I'm so sorry to come barging in like this but I panicked. Thank God Curtis was here.' As if he heard her talking about him Curtis walked into the kitchen.

'Well whoever it was Lara, they're long gone. There was a pot plant toppled over but nothing else. Did you manage to get a look at him?'

'No I didn't I really just felt someone staring at me and then when I went to the curtain to take a look I heard footsteps going down the stairs and the pot plant falling. I must have scared him off.' Lara accepted the tea that Janie offered her and took a small sip of the hot liquid.

'I don't think he'll be back but can you come into work tomorrow and I'll write up a report and talk to Sarge about what the next step will be. Will you be alright staying there tonight, or do you want to stay here?'

'This is so annoying. I'm not going to be intimidated by a Peeping Tom. Honestly that's one of the reasons I left Melbourne, to get away from this sort of thing. I'm not going to run anymore,' she said, sounding more confident than she felt.

'So do you think this could be related to what happened in Melbourne? Someone, following you up here?' Curtis filled a glass of water and took a big swallow. Lara couldn't help her gaze lingering on his Adam apple as it bobbed up and down. Janie looked at one then the other and said, 'Can you go and put some clothes on Curtis, you're practically naked.'

'Oh of course sorry,' he laughed, 'I was asleep when I heard the door and just grabbed the nearest thing.' As he left the kitchen Lara looked down at her own clothes and realised she had on her silk shorts and a tight white singlet top with no bra.

'Hey, I'd better get going too, thanks again for the tea and sympathy. I'll catch you tomorrow,' she said, walking over to the sink and tipping out the last little bit of tea. She gave Janie a smile and wave of thanks as she headed towards the front door.

'Hey wait Lara, I'll walk you home.' Curtis came out of his bedroom pulling his t-shirt over his head. He opened the front door and headed out across the yard until he came to her stairs. Using his phone as a torch, he made his way to her door. Lara followed behind glad that he had suggested coming with her, it was a moonless night and the yard and surrounds were in total darkness.

'Well, thanks Curtis. I'm so sorry about this,' she smiled weakly in the mellow light.

'You know what, I'll talk to Steve Curry our electrician about putting sensor lights in here and on the balcony. And you are no bother Lara, but I will come in and give you my number if that's okay, then you can just ring me if you hear anything or get scared.'

'Thanks, that makes me feel so much better. I really appreciate this,' she said, opening her door and turning on the hall light.

'Look, if this is something to do with your past you know you can trust me, right,' he said, reaching up and putting a warm hand on her shoulder. The tingle that went through her body was electric. How could one touch change her whole nervous system from static to charge? She willed the hand to caress her soft skin, but Curtis had other ideas. He dropped his hand to his phone and blue toothed his number to hers, turned swiftly and called out, 'Lock the door behind me.'

Lara leant against the cool wood of the now locked door and pushed all thoughts of Curtis away. She just couldn't afford to go down that particular rabbit hole again so soon. Josh had ruined her for love and there was no way that she was ever going to dangle her heart out there again, no matter how good looking and kind the prize may be.

That night Lara was awoken by a sound coming from the street. She rolled over half asleep, got out of her bed and went over to the curtain to look out the window. What seemed to be a large semi-trailer was rolling down the main town with its lights off. As it went past the street light Lara could just make out the signage 'Olsen Brothers'. *That's strange, why no lights,* she thought. The semi came to a stop as the driver lit up a cigarette, illuminating his whole cabin for just a second. Lara saw a man hunched over the wheel; he wore a dark hoodie. Slowly the truck rumbled off down the main street heading towards Talbot.

6

Chapter Six

The next morning Lara threw on her leggings and a 'save the bees' t-shirt and decided to push out the negative energy threatening to implode inside of her. It had taken her a long time to get to where she was and there was no way thoughts of Josh and Peeping Toms were going to set her back. She remembered some of the techniques that her psychologist had taught her to stay calm, one of them being physical exercise. Lara hit the sidewalk and headed towards the riverbed. With AC/DC screaming 'Thunderstruck' in her ear pods, Lara pounded towards the park, brown pigtail swinging in her wake. *I am stronger than this, I am stronger than this...*became her mantra as her Nike's bit into the red dust.

Lara slowed down to catch her breath. She placed her hands on her knees and took several deep breaths. She then reached up to the sky, opening her diaphragm and letting her breathing slow. *Breathe in breathe out, breathe in breathe out, I am stronger than this.* Her surroundings calmed her. The warble of the magpie had always been a sound that Lara loved and from the giant ghost gums around her the sound reverberated through the bush. *I am stronger than this...*

Turning back towards the town Lara reflected on the past few days that she had been in River Bend. Not without its dramas; firstly, a roadkill and now a Peeping Tom. Well, it was not going to ruin this new part of her life. She felt somehow connected to the community and was excited to meet her new boss this afternoon at the school where he was going to do a handover of her new grade. Lara had received a list of her students when she was in Melbourne and had already set up colourful class rainbow fish labels and a cute door display, 'Welcome to 1/ 2 B! We all swim together in this grade'.

Lara called into the IGA for some breakfast cereal and a well-deserved Red Bull. She pulled her phone out of her pocket ready to pay.

'Good morning Pearl how are you today?' smiled Lara, looking down at her phone.

'Oh love its Shirl not Pearl,' laughed Shirl not Pearl.

'Jeez Pearl served me yesterday. I'm sorry but I just can't seem to pick you two apart. I don't mean to be rude,' stuttered Lara, quickly looking up and staring at Shirl with what she hoped was an apologetic face.

'Oh my giddy aunt that's okay love, you and everyone else in this town. Now what about your Peeping Tom last night? You must have had quite a shock,' said Shirl, lowering her voice.

'How did you hear about that?' questioned Lara, confused.

'Well, Derek Harkness told me when he delivered the papers early this morning. It's true pet, small towns have the biggest mouths. I was so concerned about you, what with your accident, and now this. You'll think the town has the devil in it.'

'No I'm perfectly okay thanks Shirl,' said Lara, feeling a bit prickly. 'I'll put this Special K and drink on my card thanks.' Lara held out her phone to pay, not quite believing that the events of last night were already town gossip. How could Curtis have done this to her? She felt like a fool. Boy was she going to give him a piece of her mind. *Trust me, he had said.*

After breakfast and a long hot shower Lara felt much better. She threw on denim shorts, a white t-shirt, and thongs. Comfortable in her normal summer attire, she walked the few blocks to the police station.

He was manning the front counter when she walked in.

'Hi Lara, how are you feeling after last night?' Curtis asked smiling up at her, his green eyes twinkling in the morning sunshine coming through the side window.

'Well, to be honest, I am a bit annoyed actually, Curtis. I thought the police took an oath or something not to spread gossip and private happenings around the town,' she said, with a little bit of sass in her voice.

'Whoa,' he said, holding up his hands as if to deflect her words. 'I've no idea what you are talking about.'

'So Pearl or Shirl,' she raised her shoulders in confusion and continued on, 'at the IGA just happens to magically know that I had a Peeping Tom visit me last night. I kind of thought that was *my* private information to share,' she emphasized the 'my' by raising her voice, 'and I've already caused enough drama and been made the centre of attention with the whole Skippy thing...'

'Stop Lara, I think you are barking up the wrong tree.'

'What is it with silly sayings in this town, honestly, barking up what tree! How then, does half the town know about my night visitor?'

'What's going on here Constable?' said a short, bald man coming from the frosted doors at the back of the office.

'Sarge, this is Lara Benton, the lady I was telling you about this morning. I'm about to take her statement,' Curtis stammered to his boss.

'Right. Good to meet you, Miss Benton. What seems to be the problem?' The Sergeant came around the desk and offered his hand for Lara to shake. It felt cold and limp in her warm hand.

'Oh no, everything's fine Sergeant.' Lara didn't want to get Curtis in trouble and he certainly could get reprimanded if he'd been spreading gossip about her.

'Sarge, I can take care of Lara's statement,' said Curtis, with a small nod of thanks towards Lara.

'Okay if you are sure, Constable. Nice to meet you girlie,' he said to Lara and turned to Curtis. 'I'm just off to interview a lady in Talbot who has had some clothing taken from her line,' he said. He gave Lara the once over as he slammed the front door of the station. *Girlie? Really, in this day and age,* thought Lara.

'Listen here *Miss Benton*, you owe me an apology.' Curtis came around and opened the door to a back office. 'As if I would spread your personal information around this town and *what* the Early twins. I don't think so.'

'Shirl or Pearl said they heard it from a Derek Harkness!' She walked through the door in front of Curtis and wished she had maybe not been so aggressive earlier. He looked so cute in his uniform that her stupid body was rebelling against her angry words.

'I think you may owe me a huge apology.' He pulled out a chair for her to sit on then sat before his computer and booted it up.

'What do you mean,' she said, screwing up her face in confusion.

'Well, when I was running around the streets looking for your Peeping Tom, putting myself in harm's way for YOU, I ran into Eric Polson walking his dog Buster and questioned him as to whether or not he had seen a man running down your steps. Guess what Lara, his neighbour is Derek Harkness. Do you think, what was it you said about small town sayings, you've got the wrong end of the stick? You've jumped in boots and all! You've thrown the baby out with the bath water.'

'That doesn't even make sense Curtis. You are just sprouting silly sayings now. Oh, I feel terrible. Please, I really appreciate that you helped me. I just assumed it was you. I'm sorry,' she said. She hoped he would understand that she had made a mistake and cursed Josh for making her mistrust all men, even good ones like Curtis.

'Never assume Lara, it makes an ass out of you and me!'

Lara's Research:

My giddy aunt: an exclamation of shock or surprise.

Barking up the wrong tree: to mistake one's object, or to pursue the wrong course to obtain it.

The wrong end of the stick: an incorrect understanding of something.

Jumped in boots and all: making every effort; no holds barred.

Throw the baby out with the bath water: you lose the good parts of something as well as the bad parts.

Assume: ass out of you and me.

7

Chapter Seven

After Lara had given her statement to Curtis she went back to her room to collect her school things. Her car still wasn't ready, but Curtis had told her that it was only a twenty-minute walk. He also offered to drive her but she felt that she had already put him out enough in the last couple of days. Lara packed her things into her backpack and took off for the school, following the main road out of town. When the school came into view, it looked like there were two main sandstone buildings in keeping with the theme of the town. There was an administrative section with play equipment at the back, and two large willow trees which gave off shade and added a touch of green to the landscape. It had a lovely country feel and Lara felt a sense of happiness wash over her. She didn't like to admit it, but the last couple of days had been pretty full on and it was nice to see that the school lived up to the picture in her mind. There was a Ford station wagon parked out the front and it looked like a couple of kids playing on the equipment. Lara headed towards the administrative building and knocked loudly calling out, 'Hello'.

Desmond O'Brien was a very, very tall man with short greying hair. He was in his late fifties and had been teaching for more than thirty years. He showed Lara to her room and explained how the interactive whiteboard worked and gave her a printout of all the passwords she would need.

Over a cup of tea, they discussed the children in her grade. There were twenty-two in total and Des knew all of them except two, little Elsie who Lara had met the day before and a new boy called Tom Wilson. Des didn't know much about him at all, just that he lived out on Bard Road, east of the township. Des told her there was one other teacher at the school and she looked after the foundation and kindergarten children.

'How many children altogether, Des?' asked Lara.

'We have twenty-four foundation and kinder kids, your twenty-two in the junior area, and I teach fifteen middles and seniors, so all up sixty-one. Not a huge school but not the smallest in the area. Talbot has the nearest primary school and they have over a hundred students plus the only high school for miles. We are financially just keeping our heads above water but the commute to Talbot is over an hour, that's two hours a day for our kids so the government is happy to keep funding us. The community is also very supportive and run lots of raffles, a yearly fete, and different bits and bobs to help pay for the little things that make this such a great school.'

When Des left with his grandchildren Lara cleaned her room and put the sign she'd made on her door. School returned after Australia Day next week so she didn't have much time to get organised. She was so excited to meet the children and finally teach. Time got away from her and it was after five when she locked her door and headed back into River Bend. As she walked along the gravel pathway at the edge of the tarmac road, she saw a mob of kangaroos bound over the dry earth. A lone wedge-tailed eagle screeched across the sky and landed on the boughs of an acacia tree. The bright blue sky was turning a darker shade of blue as late afternoon appeared. It was so pretty that Lara stopped to admire the scene in front of her, awestruck by its beauty, it was like something out of a travel magazine. It was moments like this that Lara wished she could draw or paint so that she could share this with the world. She took her phone out of her back pocket and took several photos, trying to capture the beauty in front of her. She was sending the pictures in a text to her mum and dad when a white Mitsubishi ute drove past her and then made a U-turn. The passenger window lowered and Curtis yelled out to her, 'Hi Lara I was hoping to catch you, do you want a lift?'

'Thanks Curtis, this backpack is certainly heavier now than when I left this afternoon.'

Lara hopped into the passenger seat and buckled her seat belt.

'Janie and I are going to the Rivy Arms for dinner if you want to join us?' Curtis put his foot on the accelerator and the ute took off along the hot tar road.

After Lara had changed into jean shorts and a daisy yellow peasant top which set off her blue eyes, she went to meet Curtis and Janie at the pub. They were sitting out under one of the colourful umbrellas. Janie's dark curly hair was tied up into a high pony tail and she was laughing at something Curtis was saying. Lara had never had a sibling and looking at the scene in front of her she wondered, not for the first time, why her mother and father stopped at her. When she'd confronted them about the lack of a brother or sister they would always laugh and say, *we made perfection in you Lara Jane so we stopped at that.* Now, as an adult, Lara realised that her parents were quite old when she was born so that probably explained her lack of a sibling and NOT perfection, because she was definitely far from perfect. She went straight to the outdoor bar and ordered a chardonnay from the good-looking Irish bartender as she could see the others already had drinks. She carried her drink over to the table and sat down smiling a hello to everyone.

'Here she is. How did you go at school today, Lara?' asked Janie, taking a sip of her beer.

'Really well. Des seems lovely and I'm looking forward to meeting all the children. I've almost got my room ready so I'm pretty happy. Cheers everyone,' said Lara, lifting her drink in a salute to her new friends.

'So I'm glad you've had a good day after the couple of terrible ones you have had. I was waiting to hear that you'd run back to the city,' laughed Curtis.

'Oh, I'm not that easily turned off, Curtis.' She picked up the menu to check out the food.

'What's this, twenty different types of parmas? That's just crazy. Mexican parmigiana, Cheesy-stuffed eggplant parmigiana, Surf & Turf parma, The Texas T, The Shamrock supreme. I am in shock,' laughed Lara, looking at the other two, gobsmacked.

'See a little backwater town can still pull out the shock treatment. People come from all over the country to try the Rivy Arms twenty parmigianas. Paddy O'Rourke bought the Riv about two years ago and has transformed it into this,' said Janie, looking over at the bar and sweeping her hands around to emphasize the space before them.

'Oh is that the cute Irish guy that served me just then,' said Lara, turning around to look at the bar as well.

'Cute hey, a bit of competition Janie dear,' laughed Curtis. 'She won't admit it Lara, but our Janie has the hots for young Paddy.'

'Oh shut up Curtis, we are not twelve anymore,' she said, batting a hand across his arm and laughing.

Just then the man himself came across to say hello. Lara could see that Janie instantly sat up a little bit straighter and nervously put a wayward curl behind her ear.

'Hi guys it's nice to see you all. Are you staying for dinner?' he said, addressing everyone but looking directly into Janie's eyes. Lara felt the spark between them.

'G'day Paddy, I don't think you've met Lara yet. She's the new primary school teacher. Lara Paddy, Paddy Lara,' said Curtis, smiling at Paddy.

'Hi Paddy you served me at the bar, it's great to meet you,' said Lara, warmly. 'I can't wait to try one of these interesting parmas, any suggestions?'

'Well I have to say my favourite is the Hawaiian, but I love cooked pineapple so... And young Janie here is the president of the "I hate cooked pineapple" club,' laughed Paddy, giving Janie a pat on the back.

'It's just not right Paddy, I've told you that pineapple is meant to be cold and fresh, not soggy and warm,' laughed Janie, draining the last of her beer.

'Hey can I get you all another round,' he said, collecting the empty glasses on their table.

'Yeah thanks Paddy,' said Curtis. 'The same again; can you put it on my tab mate? Ah, Lara, what are you drinking?'

'Are you sure Curtis, I can get mine,' she said, not wanting to take advantage of anyone.

'Of course not Lara, the same again I'm assuming,' he said, giving Paddy a nod.

After dinner Janie went inside to talk to some of the locals and Lara sat back in her chair enjoying the small breeze that wafted through the beer garden.

'I am as full as a goog,' she said, rubbing her belly.

'It's pretty good grub here that's for sure,' said Curtis, playing with a Rivy Arms coaster.

'So were you and Janie born and bred here?' she asked, wanting to know more about this man in front of her.

'Yeah well, we grew up here but left when we were younger. Janie came back about five years ago and I came back after I'd finished at the academy,' he said.

'Where did you go?'

'We went to stay with an aunty of ours past Melbourne; Mornington, have you heard of it?' he replied.

'Oh yes, my family would often go to the beach there. It's beautiful. I grew up in Mt Waverley, near the Police Academy actually. So why did your family leave?' She noticed that his green eyes waivered a bit and his brows pushed together in thought.

'Well there you are, Curtis, I've been looking for you. You are not going to believe it, but someone's been poking around my backyard and every pair of undies I own are gone,' said a very unhappy Marg.

8

Chapter Eight

After dinner Lara sat outside having a cuppa when she saw Curtis pull up out the front.

'Hey Curtis,' she called down from the balcony and waved, 'do you want a cuppa?'

He bounded up the stairs two at a time and came and sat opposite her on the outdoor setting.

'Nah, I'm good, thanks Lara. Marg plied me with tea and cake. I couldn't fit another thing in.'

'So did the snowdropper leave any clues? Size nine shoe prints, or a half-smoked cigarette,' laughed Lara. For some reason she started thinking about the semi-trailer from last night. 'Hey Curtis, what do you know about the Olsen brothers?' she said, as her eyebrows came together in thought.

'Well, not that much really. I knew them when I was a kid. Old man Olsen ran the business for years before he passed away last year. He left it to his two sons, Bart and Cameron. The boys left River Bend when they were still in primary school because their parents broke up. From memory no one was surprised; old man Olsen had a bit of a reputation for being a mean bastard. Mrs. Olsen took off one morning and just moved them all to the city. Nobody in town ever saw them again until they arrived for the funeral and stayed. But honestly, I've never been in the shop since I go to the Bunnings in Talbot. I'm actually surprised that the two brothers can make a go of it here in River Bend. Why the interest?'

'Oh, silly really, but all this talk of weird things has made me remember something else that happened last night,' she said.

'Yeah, go on what?' he asked, with a quizzical look.

'I saw one of their semi-trailers going down main street late last night with its headlights off and I'm pretty sure that the driver was the guy staring up at me when I was on the balcony yesterday. You know the one in the black hoodie that I told you about this morning in my statement.'

'Maybe he just didn't want to wake everyone,' he said, lifting his shoulders in confusion. 'Yeah, it's a bit strange... Thanks for the heads up. Another weird thing happening in this town. Did you get a better look at his face? Like, could you identify any features?'

'Nah, it was too dark and the cab only lit up for a moment. But I am nearly one hundred percent sure that it was hoodie guy. Anyway getting back to Marg, were there any clues?' she asked, stretching out her long legs.

She noticed Curtis looking down at her bare brown legs and then turn away to stare out at the street.

'Nothing at all. This guy leaves nothing behind, no clues, but I'm starting to work out a bit of a pattern, even if Sarge thinks it's all a waste of time.'

'That Sarge of yours is certainly a piece of work. *Girlie,* really,' said Lara, shuddering at the memory. 'He seriously needs to get with the times.'

'I sometimes think he does it for shock value or to make himself look silly. He is definitely an interesting person to work with. So different from my old Sarge.'

'Well, it worked because if he calls me girlie again I'm going to give him a piece of my mind. You mentioned your old boss the other day. It's such a shame you didn't get a nicer boss Curtis. It helps to have someone in leadership that you trust and respect. That's how I feel about Des. He's such a good guy. Now I've taken us off track again. You were telling me about the pattern you have worked out.'

'It's early days yet but that information you gave me about the semi-trailer was very interesting. I'm going to do some digging on the Olsen brothers. Thanks for the heads up.' He stood up and stretched, exposing a tiny bit of skin above his jean shorts that Lara just couldn't help staring at. This man did things to her body that she thought had long been dried up. Licking her dry lips, she stared up at him.

'Okay, good night Lara,' he headed towards the stairs but he turned back. 'Oh, I nearly forgot to tell you about the Australia Day picnic we hold every year for River Bend Primary. It's a fundraising event with a maker's market and food trucks. Janie and I are volunteering on the barbeque,' he said, and disappeared down the stairs. She swore his eyes lingered on her lips.

Cowering in her bed she heard the shower turn off and the bathroom door burst open. Josh stood there naked except for a towel pulled low around his waist, water dripped down his torso. He yelled 'Get out of bed now.'

Buzz buzz, buzz buzz. Waking from a fitful sleep it took Lara a few seconds to realise where she was. Buzz buzz, buzz buzz, *what is that annoying noise,* slowly her mind registered and she reached over and grabbed her phone. 'Hello,' she said groggily.

'Good morning, Lara. Sorry to wake you so early but I've just finished your car and you can pick it up anytime today,' said a very chipper Bob.

'Oh, yeah, um thanks Bob, I appreciate it. I'll see you in a little bit.' She hung up and tried to push all thoughts of Josh from her mind. She fell back onto the pillow and covered her eyes with her arm, trying to push the tears back in. Would she ever move on from what happened to her back then? She had really hoped that a new beginning would be the making of her, but drama just seemed to be following her around. All she wanted was a peaceful life. Surely that wasn't too big a wish. Slowly Lara rolled out of bed and threw on her leggings, *I'll run it out,* she thought. Putting in her ear buds and pressing play on her phone,

Midnight Oil's, 'Beds are burning' invaded her head. She slammed her front door and headed down the stairs two at a time.

9

Chapter Nine

After a brutal forty-five minute run, Lara stopped outside the mechanics. Her Pulsar was parked outside gleaming in the early morning sunshine. She went in and paid her account and grabbed her keys, thanking Bob for the great job he had done. Just as she was about to get in the car she noticed the 'open' sign out the front of the Olsen Brothers Hardware and Feed Store. *Hmm, I might just pop in and have a look around,* she thought to herself. A small bell rang above her head when she opened the door. At first, there didn't seem to be anyone around, but then she heard some noises coming from the back of the building. It was one of those old-fashioned shops out of the seventies; dark, drab, with dust moats flying through the air outlined against the dirty front windows. Stock seemed to be piled up on the floor willy, nilly. *Definitely nothing inviting to see here.* She went to the closest aisle and perused the items. Nails, screws, light bulbs… Not really her cup of tea but she made her way further into the shop and stopped when she heard what sounded like a heated discussion coming from an office at the back of the store.

'You just tell that bloody driver of yours to stick to the plan and stop gallivanting all over town sneaking into peoples…wait what was that?' Lara had accidentally kicked over a metal bucket laying on the ground. She kind of recognised one of the voices but wasn't sure where from. She quickly walked back down the aisle towards the main counter, her heart pounding, and called out. 'Anyone here?' From the back of the building a large dark-haired man came out of the office towards her. He looked to be in his late twenties. She thought she saw a shadowy figure sneak out through the back door but the dark-haired man quickly blocked her view.

Very slowly he bent down and righted the overturned bucket staring at her all the while. He came down the aisle towards her.

'Oh, hi I'm just looking for some, ah, cat food.' That was all she could come up with at short notice.

'Yeah, they're in aisle three, halfway up on the left,' he said gruffly, and looked behind as though he was making sure the other person had left. Lara headed towards the cat food and selected the nearest one and took it back to the counter to pay.

'What sort of cat have you got?' he said, looking her up and down with a sneer.

'Ah,' she said, confused, and then conjured up a cat story, 'Oh it's a stray that keeps coming to my door.'

'That's kind of you. Are you new in town? I haven't seen you around before,' he asked, giving her the once over suspiciously, staring directly at her bust region. She felt an uncomfortable shiver go down her backbone.

'Yes, I'm Lara,' she said, reaching out her hand to shake, but feeling like not giving him too much information.

He ignored her hand and just said. 'That'll be five dollars and thirty cents.' She stared at him in confusion and then realised he was talking about the cost of the cat food. She passed her phone over and tapped, taking the can and heading out the door. Once she was safely outside, she took a deep breath of relief that she was free of the suffocating building and the stare of that awful man.

Lara jumped into her car and threw the cat food on the seat beside her. She started up the engine and did a quick U-turn heading towards the Cozy, Cup & Wares. She parked in a spot out the front and made her way up to her room. Once safe inside she texted Curtis to meet her after his shift, at the Rivy Arms Hotel.

He was sitting at the bar talking to Paddy when she arrived.

'Hey, what do you want to drink Lara?' he said, waving towards her.

'Oh um, maybe a G&T, thanks Curtis. Hi Paddy,' she said, taking a seat next to him at the bar.

'Hi Lara, how's things?' said Paddy, getting down the gin from the top shelf.

'Yeah, good thanks Paddy,' she replied.

After Paddy had deposited her drink, he left to serve some other customers at the other end of the bar.

'So I loved hearing from you today Lara, but I've got the feeling you've something on your mind,' said Curtis, taking a big swig of his beer.

After she had told him about her visit to the hardware and feed store, and what she had overheard, she took a long sip of her gin.

'Jeez Lara, do you think whoever was talking knew that you had overheard some of what they were saying?'

'Nah, I honestly don't think so. I made it back to the counter before the owner came out of the back door. But I'm telling you Curtis I have heard that voice before.' she said, shaking her head in frustration.

'What did he look like again?'

'Well, I only saw his outline and he was kind of short and stocky.'

'That could be half the male population of River Bend I'm afraid.' Curtis reached for his beer and then continued, 'So we are thinking that they were talking about the snowdropper, sneaking around in peoples... Maybe he was going to say backyard or something. I wished you could have got a look at the guy but never mind. I'm just wondering how we could find out the name of Olsen's employees. Maybe I could contact my detective mate in Talbot, he could certainly look into it, I'm sure. The snowdropper could definitely be the guy you saw driving the 'Olsen Brothers' semi the other night and they have got wind that he's been up to no good. But what's the plan he's meant to be sticking to, mmm, interesting?'

'Do you want the same again, my shout this time?' said Lara, calling Paddy over and ordering their drinks. This time they headed over to a private table in the corner.

'Are you going to tell Sarge what I overheard or keep it to yourself?' she asked, knowing that Curtis didn't really have the full support of his boss where the snowdropper case was involved.

'No, I don't think I will at the moment. I just wish you knew who was talking to the Olsen brother. From your description it sounds like it was the older one, Bart. Cameron has a distinct scar above his right eye. He didn't have a scar, did he?'

'No scar, Curtis. He just gave off a really sinister vibe, I'm afraid. Sent the chills down my spine,' she said, giving a bit of a shiver as she remembered the feeling she'd had earlier.

'Well, I definitely don't want you going back into that place, Nancy Drew. You can step back from the investigation and let a real professional deal with it,' he said, realising that Lara had got a real fright from her encounter with the sleazy Bart and trying to make light of the situation.

'Absolutely, Goldie. My time as a detective is over, done and dusted as Shirl or Pearl would like to say,' she laughed, feeling a little better that Curtis was taking her concern seriously.

'Umm, Goldie,' he said, lifting one eyebrow into a perfect arch and staring intently into her eyes.

'Oh, I didn't think I had said that out loud, sorry. I have a habit of giving nicknames to people,' she said, as a blush of hot red moved up from her cheeks.

'That was my nickname at the academy. I haven't heard it in a while,' he said, finishing the dregs of his beer.

'Well then Goldie it is,' she laughed, just as a local came over selling raffle tickets for a meat tray.

'The meat tray is donated by the local butcher and the money raised goes to the River Bend footy club,' Curtis said, in an exploration of why one of the locals was carrying around a huge tray of sausages, chops, hamburgers and steaks.

'My God if I won, I'd have to give half of it away. It would never fit in my small freezer,' laughed Lara, looking at the enormous amount of meat.

'I'd be more than willing to share it with you Lara,' he said, with a tilt of his head and a twinkle in his eye.

'Does that mean you'd help cook it as well as eat it?' she teased back.

'Love to but let's not get ahead of ourselves. Old mate has sold quite a few tickets by the look of it and I'm not particularly lucky when it comes to River Bend raffles. I just missed out on the crochet rug that the Early twins made when the CWA held their annual craft market. I spent a fortune trying to get that rug,' he shook his head as if it was the saddest thing ever. 'Hey you don't know how to crochet do you...?'

'Not on your nelly. I don't crochet, knit or change nappies. I am, however, quite lucky when it comes to raffles. I got first prize in grade three for the Easter raffle, we had chocolates till Christmas and, even better, I got the second prize for the Bunnings raffle. It was super exciting: nails, screws, picture hooks, a packet of sugar soap, compost and plant fertilizer and even a car wash set. My dad was rapt,' she laughed. 'Me, not so much.'

'Now that's a raffle. Damn you are lucky, what I wouldn't give to win that raffle.'

10

Chapter Ten

'Okay you can absolutely say NO to what I'm about to ask you, Zumba's not everyone's cup of tea,' said an over excited Pearl, when Lara called into the IGA the next morning for milk and bread. 'But I have to tell you that Marg would be over the moon to get a new member on Saturday morning, even if it was just for a squiz.'

'It sounds like fun and I'm not doing anything Saturday morning so I'd love to come for a *squiz.*' Lara emphasised the word squiz.

'Leave it with me pet and I'll book'em Danno!' She handed Lara her cotton bag, smiling happily, almost as if she'd sucked in another sucker. Lara wondered just how productive this Zumba was going to be if an older lady like Marg was taking the lesson. And also, who the hell was Danno. *Wait, maybe Marg isn't that old, it could be just the grey hair. I'll have to ask Janie.* Now that she thought about it, Marg had an amazing figure, she was medium height and slim, with pale skin and dark eyes. The few times that Lara had seen her around town she always dressed fashionably in tailored jeans and nice printed tops. Yes, it was definitely the grey hair that let her down. Lara headed to the Cozy, Cup & Wares to see Janie and grab a hot drink.

'Hi Janie,' she waved, as she walked into the cheerful area that Janie had made. She'd arranged throw rugs over chairs and there were tables with books on them for her customers to read or flick through. With the velvet couches and Mediterranean tiled tables, it was a welcoming space. It was like a home away from home and Lara had taken to curling up on a couch with one of Janie's special hot chocolates to read her favourite romance novels. There were about three tables of people having breakfast so Janie wasn't rushed off her feet. On the weekends she employed a young girl from the town to help take the orders and clear the tables. Lara walked up to the counter and plonked down on one of the mismatched stools that dotted the area.

'So please tell me you do Zumba on a Saturday morning?' she asked, playing with one of the sugar sachets.

'Yes, I wouldn't miss it. Luckily for me the ladies start the class at 8.45 so I'm back to open up by 10,' she laughed. 'Hot choc?' Janie got her stainless-steel milk jug ready.

'Oh yes please Janie, extra hot thanks.'

'Yes, I know your order now, skinny, extra hot. You are one of the less demanding people that order here. Now I always have to have almond milk, soy milk, caramel extract, hazelnut, vanilla, even, believe it or not, someone came in the other day and wanted a coconut milk cappuccino, honestly,' she laughed, throwing back her head and showing her perfectly even white teeth. Today she was wearing a really cute denim overall ensemble, cut off as shorts, with a bright tie-dye t-shirt underneath. Janie always looked so bohemian and natural. She was one of those people who could just throw something together and look great. Lara always struggled with her outfits, never feeling trendy enough. She was happy to downplay it with plain t-shirts, denim shorts, or her favourite comfortable jeans. Josh didn't make it easy for her either, he'd never complimented her on a new dress or a new pair of shoes she may have worn. Just for that extra added touch Janie had a pink carnation pushed behind her ear showing off her dark curls. She noticed Lara looking at it. 'Do you like my flower? That adorable little Harper gave it to me this morning when the girls and their mother came in for milkshakes. I told Tiffany about Zumba so I'm hoping she'll come as well. It must be lonely for her with her husband away so much. Now I don't want to put too much pressure on you, but a few of us meet once a month and do book club. I see you reading quite a bit so let me know if you are interested. It's very casual and there is wine involved,' she laughed, handing Lara her hot chocolate.

'Janie I would love that. Reading is my passion. What book are you doing?'

'Well, it's a historical fiction called *I remember you*. I have a copy here you can borrow; I couldn't put it down and finished it in a week. You will love it.'

'Awe thanks Janie, you're an angel. I'd love to read it and join the book club if the others will let me.'

'They will be thrilled, trust me.' Janie winked and went to serve a customer who had just walked in.

Lara took her hot chocolate and new book over to one of the couches out in the back courtyard. She could hear the noisy miners in the flowering gum that divided the courtyard of Janie and Curtis's cottage. Their war cries reverberated around the sandstone walls of the old building as they all took off to find something tasty in the Gold's backyard. She sipped her hot sugary drink and got lost in the pages of her new novel as the sun filled courtyard warmed her body as well as her soul. She felt content and happy for the first time in a long time. She had a lovely home, a great job and boss, and now she had Zumba and a book club. She was part of the community and it felt great.

'Well, hello there, do you mind if I join you?' She looked up to find Curtis standing there holding a mug of something hot. Her tummy did funny little flip flops and her heart seemed to miss a beat, as she looked up at him. His dark curls were in their usual state of disarray, like he had been using his hand as a comb. He was casually dressed in denim shorts and a grey and black striped t-shirt that showed off the definition around his biceps. She smiled at him and he jumped down opposite her on the matching couch.

'So, Zumba and book club hey. This town really has its claws into you now. You know once you sign up you can never get out of it. Those ladies will hound you and hunt you down,' he laughed and took a sip of his coffee.

'Okay a bit dramatic but I'm hearing you. Luckily for me I know the local cop and I'm sure he will protect me,' she batted her eyes at him and laughed. *Oh my God, am I flirting with him,* she thought.

'You have a great laugh,' he said, and turned a shade of red as he realised he'd said out loud what he possibly hadn't intended to.

Adorable, Lara thought and said, 'Well thank you kind sir, I'm glad you like my laugh. Now please tell me you participate in Zumba. I need a friend as my dancing skills are questionable,' she feigned an innocent look, closed her book and put it on the table between them.

'Not on your nelly. You're on your own Miss Lara. And when it's Janie's turn to host a book club I'm out of there. Trust me those nights can get a bit wild,' he laughed.

'Really, sounds like fun to me.' She loved the easy banter that they had. It just seemed to come naturally. Lara really didn't have that much experience in talking to the opposite sex. She'd spent her early twenties in lockdown with a very temperamental Josh. She never felt really comfortable talking to him, which was weird because they'd been going out together for two years, one of those living together because of stupid lockdown rules. Josh said he couldn't be without her and insisted that she move in with him. Timid little Lara had done what Josh wanted. Well, this is a different Lara now. River Bend Lara, she laughed to herself.

'What are you thinking? Your lips just curled up into a smile,' said Curtis, leaning forward staring at her.

'I was actually thinking about what a new start feels like.'

'And what does a new start feel like Lara?' he asked, tilting his head slightly as if he was really interested in her answer. Not brushing her off like Josh would do.

'Well, it feels like this Goldie,' she said, sweeping her hands in an arc to indicate the small courtyard. 'A wonderful new place and some really lovely new friends, book club and Zumba, that's what a new start in River Bend means to me.'

<u>Lara's Research:</u>

Book 'em Danno: It comes from the television series Hawaii Five-O and became quite a saying in the '70s and '80s. Danny was one of the police officers and his superior would say, 'Book 'em Danno' at the end of the show or, to instruct him to arrest the suspects. In current usage, if people wanted to book an event they would say, 'Book 'em Danno'.

11

Chapter Eleven

Lara woke up bright and early for the Australia Day celebrations. She had promised Janie that she would help with the food preparations so after showering and putting on her jean shorts and an Australia Day tank top, she headed downstairs to find Curtis and Janie prepping the barbeque food.

'Here Lara, grab that knife and start splitting the rolls.' Janie pointed to a crate of rolls on the bench. 'Cute outfit.'

'How come she gets rolls and I get the bloody onions?' said Curtis, turning around to face Lara, sporting a snorkel and mask.

'You just look so wrong on so many different levels. If I had Facebook, I'd definitely put a photo of you on it. It would make everyone laugh and give silly cat videos a run for their money.' Lara started cutting the rolls while shaking her head at Curtis's antics.

'Well, you must be the only person over thirteen and under seventy-five that doesn't have Facebook,' he laughed.

'Not everyone needs to document their life step by step for the world to follow.' She regretted bringing it up. Lara had deleted her account when she left Melbourne just to try and stay a step ahead of Josh.

They piled all the food into Curtis's ute and headed off to the river to set up for the celebrations. The three of them sat closely together with Lara, piggy in the middle, rubbing thighs with Curtis. Staring straight ahead she tried to regulate her breathing. Every time his skin touched hers tiny sparks flew through her body heightening her senses.

Her mind was in turmoil. *What was happening here? She'd come for a new start not a new relationship.* Apparently her body had a different agenda.

The picnic area where Elsie and Harper were staying had been transformed into a market extravaganza. There were marquees of different shapes and colours everywhere, with people carrying goods to trestle tables. Food trucks had started arriving and Des O'Brien was there setting up the barbeque area where Lara had also volunteered to work. *So, this is what it's like to be part of a country community,* thought Lara, waving to a hyped up Elsie and Harper.

It was lovely working side by side with Curtis. She saw how respected he was in the community and how everyone knew him and Janie. When the lunch rush was over Des shooed them away to go and join in the celebrations. They ended up drinking beers at the Rivy Arms portable beer garden down by the dry riverbed.

'You should see this place when the river runs, Lara. When Janie and I were kids, see that old willow over there, that's the bend in the river that our town is named after. You can't really see it when the bed is dry but when the water flows it's an awesome sight.' He pointed to a large tree at the riverbank. 'Anyway, we used to climb up on the willow's boughs and,' he reached over closer to her, 'see that old rope, we would swing each other out and jump into the rushing water. God it was so much fun.' His bare arm brushed against hers and sent a shiver down her spine, causing the hairs on her arm to practically stand up with static electricity. His green eyes shone with nostalgia and she was so close to him that the brown flecks in his eyes seemed to spark. Her gaze moved to his full lips and it was all she could do to stop herself from wetting her thumb and sliding it over his bottom lip. *Oh God, to feel his mouth moulded onto her mouth, teeth grinding against her lower lip,* it took all of her willpower not to physically moan out loud.

'Come on Lara lets go and take a look at the market,' he said, obviously not realising the physical affect his proximity was having on her. He reached over and casually grabbed her hand, pulling her up out of the deck chair she was in. They roamed through the market looking at candles, earrings, books and an assortment of honeys, chutneys and pickles.

'Every stall owner has paid fifty dollars to be here, and that money goes directly to the school. Plus, the money we make from the barbeque, less the food of course,' he said, waving to different people and families as he went. 'Here, can you hold my chutney while I just go over and check out the portable toilets.' He pointed to a nearby tree in the shade and Lara headed towards it. Lara stood under the canopy watching the people of River Bend enjoying the glorious weather and festivities.

She sensed more than saw somebody walk up behind her and then heard a gravelly voice say.

'So, how's that stray cat going?'

She whipped around to be face to face with Bart Olsen. Her heart leapt into her mouth.

'Well, believe it or not the damn thing hasn't shown up since I bought that can of cat food. A waste of money. Do you give returns for unused goods?' she said, sounding more confident than she felt.

'Nah, sorry you'll just have to wear the cost, I'm afraid,' he laughed, but the smile did not reach his eyes. 'So I've been doing a bit of poking around. You're the new schoolteacher, living above that cafe in town.'

Lara felt distinctly uneasy as he spoke to her, and even more annoyed that he knew where she was living. *Damn small towns, I bet those gossipy Early twins have something to do with this*, she thought, rather unkindly.

'You can't keep anything a secret in a small town,' she said, lifting her chin in defiance as she hated the way this man made her feel.

'Yeah, especially when new meat moves in.' He leered at Lara, stepping in even closer and invading her personal space. He put his head down staring at her legs and then slowly moved his eyes all the way up her body to her face. She took a large step back to reclaim her space but still managed to feel a shiver go up her backbone as she clenched her hands together into fists to stop them from shaking.

'Thanks Lara, I'll take the bag.' Curtis stood beside her and put a protective hand at the small of her back.

'G'day Bart, how's things?' he said, standing up tall and towering over the smaller man.

Bart's eyes narrowed and his mouth turned down in a scowl as he looked at Curtis.

Yeah, I'm good, thanks *mate*. How are things going with you?' he sneered. 'I heard you'd come back to the fold. I thought it may have been too painful to come back here given your family history.'

'No Bart, my family history is in the past,' he said. Lara could feel his hand stiffen against her back.

To try and defuse the situation Lara quickly turned to Bart and said, 'Well nice seeing you again, come on Curtis, we have to meet Janie at the beer tent.' She grabbed his hand and pulled him in the direction they had come from.

'Oh my God he is an awful man,' she said, walking towards the river, sensing that Curtis's mind was definitely not on the celebrations anymore.

When they got back to the tent Lara went and ordered them both a drink and carried it over to a table under one of the flowering gums.

'Here you go Curtis, are you okay? Bart seemed to hit a nerve.' She passed him a cold beer and put down a packet of crisps to share.

'Yeah, look it's nothing Lara. He just managed to get under my skin. There is definitely something going on with him but as yet I have no idea what it could be. Anyway, let's forget about him and just enjoy your last day of freedom before you start your new school year tomorrow. Are you excited?' He smiled up at her and seemed to physically shed all thoughts of Bart Olsen and the comment about his family.

'Gosh, excited, nervous, terrified, you name it and I'm feeling it,' she laughed.

'Those kids are gonna love you Lara, how could they not,' he said, blushing shyly.

'Why thank you Goldie, that's very kind of you to say. Let's hope they love me and don't eat me alive,' she said, feeling a warm glow start in her toes and rise up to her heart. *What a sweet man,* she thought, smiling secretly to herself.

'You certainly do run with a nickname,' he laughed back at her. She desperately wanted to tell him how much she loved his laugh, but for once held back.

'Well, hello there you two,' said Pearl or Shirl, selling what looked like raffle tickets.

'It's five dollars a book, you have to be in it to win it,' said one of the twins with a wink.

Lara reached for her wallet and pulled out a ten dollar note and asked for two books.

'When is it drawn ladies?' she asked, not ready to try her luck at using a name yet.

'Des O'Brien is drawing it in about half an hour.'

'I'll also have two books, thanks Pearl. Not that I like my chances since Lara has the luck of the Irish about her when it comes to winning raffles.' Curtis handed over the money and winked at her. Lara laughed at the 'in' joke and then looked from one to the other waiting to see if Curtis had named the twin correctly. No one corrected him, much to her amazement. She scrutinized the women in front of her and just could not work it out.

'Any news on the snowdropper front Curtis? I really need my undergarments back sometime,' said the one Curtis had called Pearl. Lara was horrified that they wanted their undies back after they had been with, she assumed, an unsavoury man.

'Nothing to report, I'm afraid Pearl,' replied Curtis.

'Hi Pearl, hi Shirl, Curtis, Lara. Heard you had signed up for Zumba Lara, good on you,' said a rather flushed Marg, coming over to the little group.

Lara once again looked at the twins to see if Marg had got their names right. No one disagreed with her.

'Yes Marg, I am really looking forward to it, and I'm loving the book club novel as well.'

'Good on you pet, we meet on the first Tuesday of the month so you have a week left to read it,' said either Pearl or Shirl. Lara still wasn't confident enough to say the names out loud.

'We're ready to start putting the tickets in the barrel if you are happy you've sold enough,' Marg said to the twins.

'I've got three left to sell and Pearl's all done,' said Shirl.

'I'll grab the last three thanks Pearl,' said Smithy, coming over to join the little group.

'How's that head of yours Lara? Let me take a quick look.' He pulled a twenty dollar note from his pocket and handed it to one of the twins; Lara had lost track of them now as they had moved position while she stood to let Smithy take a look at her head.

'Healing beautifully my girl,' he patted her gently on the shoulder, 'terrible ordeal for you. When are you starting at the school?' he asked.

'Tomorrow. And thanks for taking such good care of me, Smithy,' she smiled up at him.

'My pleasure, treasure,' he said, with the slightest tilt of his head.

'So anyway everyone, are we ready to get the raffle tickets organised? We have to break them up and put them in the barrel,' said a twin.

Feeling very brave Lara replied. 'I'll help you Shirl,' and held her breath.

'You're a duffer love, its Pearl,' laughed Pearl.

'I just don't get it. How come I'm the only one that can't pick you ladies apart,' said Lara, in frustration.

With that everyone just laughed and gave a bit of a knowing nod.

'Hang on, are you all taking the mickey out of me?' she laughed, looking around at the little group of smiling faces.

Lara's research

You have to be in it to win it: you can't win if you haven't bought a ticket.

Duffer: silly, slow to learn, incompetent person.
Taking the Mickey: playing a joke on someone.

12

Chapter Twelve

After they had helped pack up, Curtis drove Lara home and helped her take all of the picnic things up the stairs. He stood on her balcony just as the sun started to set and leave a red glow over everything.

'Well Lara, thanks again for all your help today. It was great and I'm sure we raised lots of money. The ladies from the CWA will announce the grand total at the Rivy Arms next Friday. It's a huge event on the River Bend calendar.'

'It's a very community orientated town, I like that,' she said, standing only inches away from him, loving the way the red splash of sunset played on his olive skin and made the tips of his curly dark hair shine a copper colour. She had to fight the urge to run her fingers through his hair and smooth down the wayward curls. His five o'clock shadow left a dark smudge over his cheeks giving him a rakish look.

They stood like that for what seemed like five minutes, but in reality, was only seconds, but my God did those seconds count. She stared into the depth of his eyes and felt transported into his very soul. *Please, please kiss me,* her traitor mind thought with longing, almost standing up on her tippy toes to make it easier. He cleared his throat and slowly reached up to touch the side of her cheek. She closed her eyes and shifted her head to the left to meet his touch and just as his fingers were about to graze her hot cheek, she was disturbed by a noise from behind him.

'I'm not interrupting anything am I Lara?' said a gruff voice.

Instantly her eyes shot open and she looked around Curtis to see Josh standing there holding an overnight bag in his hand.

'Josh! What the hell are you doing here?' she said, in complete amazement.

'Well that's not the welcome I was expecting from my fiancé.'

'Don't you mean ex-fiancé,' she said, as the shock of seeing him again started to sink in.

'Umm, look I'll leave you two to your reunion if you're okay with that Lara?' said Curtis, looking from one to the other and waiting for Lara to let him know if she was happy for him to go and to be left alone with this guy. He widened his eyes facing her and gave a little nod as if to say... I'll stay if you want me to.

'Yes, yes of course go Curtis, I know you have an early start tomorrow. Thanks again for helping me get my stuff home. I will see you during the week, I'm sure,' she said, giving Josh a glare from behind Curtis.

With that Curtis walked past Josh giving him a death stare as a warning to keep things amicable.

When he had left she turned to Josh. 'How the hell did you find me and what are you doing here? We left things said and done before I came away. What the hell has given you the right to come chasing me all the way to River Bend when you know how I feel? I can't be any more honest than that,' she said, facing the man that she had once loved, or thought she had loved.

'Come on Lara, you are not really going to throw everything we had over one silly mistake,' he walked towards her with his arms outstretched.

'Silly mistake, is that what you call what you did to me? No, I have definitely not changed my mind and just stop right there.' She placed her hand out in front of her in a stop sign position. 'If you come any closer, I swear I'll scream this place down.'

'But Lara...'

'No buts Josh, I want you to leave *now*!' Lara rushed inside and locked the door before he could come any closer. She leaned against the cool wood and tried to stop her body from shaking. Thankfully he left straight away. She couldn't have stood the thought of him making an embarrassing scene, like banging on the door or yelling abuse. What with the kangaroo, Peeping Tom, and now an abusive ex, the town would have a field day. *Honestly,* she thought to herself with tears falling down her cheeks, *why is he here? What the hell does he want?* She had tried so hard to get away from him many times during the lockdown and it was the last straw when he ... Anyway, she didn't want to think about that right now. She had an enormous day tomorrow and she was damned if Josh was, once again, going to ruin things for her.

The next morning Lara clambered into her car and headed towards the school. She'd had a terrible sleep thanks to Josh and was definitely in need of something else to focus on. Her little grade was exactly what she needed to ease her worry and by lunchtime she was feeling a lot more positive.

The first week flew by for Lara. She hadn't seen Josh around so concluded that he had headed back to Melbourne. *Good riddance,* she thought. That Friday night, after the Australia Day picnic, she headed to the Rivy Arms to find out how much the town had raised for her school. Unfortunately, she hadn't seen Curtis all week and was feeling very flat about that. As she walked in, she was greeted warmly by Marg and Smithy who had commandeered a large table at the front of the pub. She took her wine over to them and sat down next to Smithy.

'How's the head love? It looks like it has healed nicely, I don't even think you will have a scar. How about your week at the school? Did you meet my grandson Eli yet?'

'Oh, it's such a fabulous place. I met Eli when I was on yard duty. He's a lovely boy, Smithy.' She took a sip of her wine and scanned the room for Curtis.

'Yes we are rather proud of our grandchildren. I have six in total. Three are here and three live in Melbourne with their mother,' he said, with a nostalgic look in his eye.

'Well Melbourne's not too far to go to visit I suppose. Do they come back here much?' she asked.

'Mainly the school holidays, but they are getting older and this little town doesn't hold their interests like it did when they were little. Oh Shirl, Pearl we're over here.' He waved to the Early twins who'd just entered the pub.

Lara looked around seeing if she could spot Curtis or Janie. She noticed Curtis at the bar talking to Paddy but there was no sign of Janie. He looked so handsome leaning up against the bar in his tight denim jeans and a well fitted black t-shirt. His curly dark hair looked damp as if he had rushed here from a quick shower after work. She had missed seeing him this week. She had hoped that they may have run into each other, but it was not to be. Suddenly her attention was caught by a familiar shape at the other end of the bar. Josh was standing there talking to someone who was partially blocked by some farmers having their Friday night bevvy. He seemed to be in deep conversation with the person. *Why on earth is he still here?* she thought angrily to herself. When the crowd dispersed, she was shocked to see that the person Josh was so engrossed in was Janie.

She jumped up from her seat and marched across the room, excusing herself as she tried to push through the crowd of people waiting to hear how much they had raised at the picnic.

'Well here she is,' greeted Janie, with a warm smile. 'I've just met your Josh and he's been telling me all about your life in Melbourne.'

'Oh that's nice,' said Lara, gritting her teeth together. 'Do you mind if I steal Josh for a moment?'

'Not at all. I'll go and grab a seat at the table. Do you want me to save you both a seat?' she asked.

'I already have one thanks Janie, and Josh won't be staying,' she said, turning towards him. 'Can I speak to you outside for a moment?'

He followed her outside. When they reached the relative quiet of the beer garden, she turned on him and asked in bewilderment,

'What the hell are you still doing here? I thought you were long gone.'

'I don't give up that easily Lara. I'm not going anywhere until you come to your senses and realise that we are meant to be together,' he grabbed her tightly around her upper arm, leaving an imprint on her soft skin.

'You are delusional Josh,' she flinched and tried to pull her arm away. 'There is no *us* and we are not meant to be together. I can't make you go but I sure as hell am not going to engage with you, so stay away from me! Now Let. Go. Of. My. Arm,' she said menacingly into his ear. A wave of panic washed over her and she pushed him hard. She would never play the victim again.

'Hey Lara, is everything okay?' Curtis appeared and quickened his pace to reach her.

'Who the hell is this guy anyway Lara, and why does he keep popping up uninvited?' said a frustrated Josh.

'Listen here *mate,* get away from her now,' said Curtis, through gritted teeth. He balled his right hand into a fist and stood inches from Josh. Curtis's six-foot four frame towered over them and she could see the intimidation creep over Josh's face. His bravado was evaporating before Lara's eyes. *Good,* she thought, secretly thanking Curtis for coming to her rescue.

'Thanks Curtis but everything's okay. I think Josh realises, once and for all, that I'd like him to leave,' she said, breathing slowly to gain her composure.

'You heard the lady,' said Curtis, staring Josh down as though with any wrong move he would pounce like a lion.

'Remember Lara, I don't give up that easily,' Josh said, and took off through the beer garden to the front of the Rivy Arms. When he was gone Lara let out a large breath of air she had been subconsciously holding.

'Oh Curtis thanks so much. I'm so sorry to get you involved in my personal dramas. I just can't believe he found out where I am,' she said, trying to hold back tears.

'Let me guess, this is the reason you left Melbourne. The thing you have been running away from?' he asked her in a kind, soft voice.

'Yes, we were engaged for a short time. A very short time. I thought he was everything I had been looking for in a boyfriend. Kind, courteous, good looking, a great job as a policeman believe it or not, and then lockdown hit and I was forced to be with him for months on end with no prospect of seeing anyone else, not even my mum and dad. I was in lockdown hell, yet he could go off to work and come home and expect a slave to be waiting for him. He changed. He became angry and even violent. The last time he hit me I high tailed it out of there and ran home. I didn't care if the cops had caught me out of curfew, I just couldn't spend another minute near him. And now he's here,' she sobbed.

Curtis drew her into a giant bear hug making soothing noises.

'The bloody bastard. You know I can organise a domestic intervention order which'll mean he can't go near you.'

'Thanks Curtis, but I am really hoping he is going to leave River Bend for good. Him being a policeman doesn't make any of this any easier,' she sighed, loving the comfort of his strong arms around her. Her hands felt the knots of muscle that rippled through his shirt. Suddenly the air was electric with energy. She desperately wanted to massage his back as he held her. She felt a warmth in the lower part of her body that shocked her with its intensity. Why did this man turn her insides to mush. She literally felt her body melting, oozing into a pile of clay waiting to be moulded by his strong hands.

Curtis's fingers started to massage her back slowly in small circles and he whispered into her ear, 'I won't let him hurt you ever again, Lara.' His breath tingled on her earlobe and she slowly turned her head to feel the scratchiness of his whiskers on her soft sensitive skin.

'Hey there you two are, the Early twins are about to share the final tally, come inside.' Janie sounded surprised to see Curtis's arms around

Lara. They broke apart as if they were teenagers caught out by their parents. Lara smoothed down her dress and followed Janie back into the pub.

She took her seat next to Smithy and reached for her wine to take a small sip. Janie, who was seated on the other side of Lara, reached over and whispered, 'Are you okay?

'I just had an awful run in with my ex. Trust me we are not together and he is the reason I left Melbourne. Running away from an abusive relationship. I can't believe he's here.'

Janie rubbed Lara's hand gently and gave her a sympathetic look.

'You're safe now lovely. Curtis won't let anything happen to you trust me.'

13

Chapter Thirteen

The next morning Lara got up nice and early and got dressed in her leggings and oversized t-shirt. She threw her dark brown hair into a high ponytail. She felt a nervous anticipation growing in her stomach, hoping like hell she wouldn't embarrass herself in front of her new friends with her uncoordinated movements. She made a slice of toast and a cup of tea and took it out to the wrought iron outdoor setting. It was a glorious Saturday morning and she revelled in the feeling of the early morning sunshine touching her skin. The sound of the morning birds chirping away in the orange flowering gums that dotted around Main Street gave her a country feeling. Josh was just a small hiccup to her new happiness, and she was annoyed with herself for giving him airtime in her mind. *New beginning Lara,* she thought as she finished her toast and tea before making her way to the CWA hall two doors up.

Marg greeted her with a huge smile. 'Lara welcome, come, come. Now find a spot and we'll do a warm up.' Hilariously, Marg was decked out in the whole Zumba attire. She had on a hot pink 'I Love Zumba' t-shirt with leopard skinned leggings and a black peaked hat with Zumba embroidered across it in the same hot pink stitching. Her runners were also fluoro pink. Lara certainly felt plain and boring in her black leggings and white top. *I might have to do some shopping,* she thought as Pearl and Shirl came in with matching fluoro orange t-shirts and black and white spotted leggings. Janie came in wearing a plain black leisure outfit and Lara let out a sigh of relief as she realised it was okay to wear anything you wanted in this class. Janie gave her a quick nod and eye raise making sure that she was feeling alright after last night's run in with Josh. 'All good this morning lovely?' she whispered.

When Tiffany arrived, she sidled up to Lara and said, 'I believe you're new as well, I'm feeling a bit nervous and out of my comfort zone?' She stood next to Lara at the back of the group.

'Yep, stick with me Tiff, I'll make you look really good,' laughed Lara, with Janie joining in.

Suddenly Marg put on her head mic and it was like a personality in-fusion.

'Welcome to Zumba ladies. Are you all ready to have some *fun* and *laughs* and get your *groove* on? Our first number is my personal favourite, Ricky Martin. Let's get our "Livin' la vida loca" on.' Marg hilariously rolled her *r*'s when she said Ricky. The music blared from the Sonos on the stage and Marg started dancing and telling her group what to do through the speaker. Lara couldn't wipe the smile off her face as she watched her friends following Marg's instructions. Marg was an excellent teacher and Lara actually felt like she could do the dance moves with a little bit of flare. In certain parts of the music everyone started 'whoop, whooping'. Not to be left out, Janie and Tiffany joined in with a loud 'whoop, whoop' and Lara had to revert to biting the side of her mouth so as not to burst out laughing. Janie looked at her and winked. It was the most joyous fun Lara had had in a long time. The hour flew by and resulted in a trickle of sweat down her spine and a sheen on her rosy cheeks. Her mouth and unused muscles were sore and stiff from smiling and moving so much.

At the end of the lesson everyone went back to the Cozy, Cup & Wares and ordered drinks all round from Sally, the young girl Janie hired for the busy Saturday rush. While Janie had a quick shower and changed, Lara helped Sally make up the orders and carried the cups out into the courtyard where half the Zumba class were eagerly talking and dissecting their dance moves. Lara was glad to see that Tiffany was talking animatedly to Marg and the local hairdresser Patsy, who Lara had been introduced to at the start of the lesson. Janie had mentioned that Tiffany was lonely, so this class was such a great idea for the both of them to meet some of the other people that lived in River Bend. When Lara passed a mocha cappuccino, a hot chocolate with extra marshmallows, and two pear and walnut muffins to two of the ladies in the group who had just worked out for an hour, she tried hard not to judge that they were undoing all their hard work.

'Curtis welcome! When are you going to join us for Zumba?' said an over enthusiastic Pearl or Shirl.

'One day ladies, one day maybe, but right now I have a half strength almond milk latte for Kylie Minogue and a double strength soy latte for Delta Goodrem,' laughed Curtis, addressing the room.

'That would be us pet,' laughed Pearl and Shirl in unison. It was a bit of a joke with the twins to change their names when they placed their cafe orders with Janie.

'What are your plans for today, Curtis?' asked Marg, looking from Curtis to Lara. *Mmm what's that about*, thought Lara, *a bit of matchmaking maybe.*

'Why do you have something in mind?' Curtis winked at Marg.

'Not for me young man, I'm way too old for you. But maybe some of the young people might want to, you know, go for a bite to eat at the Rivy,' she said, looking directly at Lara.

'Well Janie and I are meeting Paddy there this afternoon and everyone is welcome. We were going to have a game of Kelly pool.'

'What's Kelly pool Curtis? It sounds like fun,' asked Patsy, picking up her skinny milk mocha cappuccino and taking a sip.

'You pick a number and then if your ball gets pocketed, you're out. Kel knows how to play. It's really just a bit of fun.'

'My mum said she'd have the kids today so Kel and I might just meet you there. Are you going to go Lara?' Patsy asked.

'I was going to do school work but that sounds like much more fun. Do you mind if I tag along, Curtis?'

'Not at all. I was going to tell you about it after your class.' He broke into a huge smile and went back to get some more orders just as Janie came into the courtyard carrying a plate of delicious looking muffins.

Lara went home feeling full and content. She was meeting Curtis and Janie at four so she decided to get her work program started for the following week. At three o'clock she had a quick shower to freshen up and put on a comfortable pair of faded jeans and a blue and white striped linen shirt that hugged her thin frame. She decided to straighten her hair and wear it out for a change. When she was happy with her look, she made her way to the hotel. The main street of River Bend was looking particularly beautiful this time of the year. The flowering gums were out in full force, their vibrant fluffy orange and red flowers contrasting with the black of the gum nuts. The sky was a brilliant blue with puffs of white clouds dotted everywhere. She was a bit early so she took a stool at the bar and chatted with Paddy. His strong Irish accent filled her with happiness as he regaled her with stories of his travels around the world. She felt glad that she had also been to some of the countries he mentioned. She must ask Curtis if he had ever travelled. He hadn't mentioned it.

Patsy was the first of the group to arrive. 'Hi Lara, Paddy, it's so nice to have a free afternoon without the kids. Lara, I don't think you have met Kel yet? Kel Lara, Lara Kel,' she said, taking the stool next to her. Lara tried not to look too surprised as she didn't realise Patsy's partner was a female. She smiled widely at Patsy and Kel.

'G'day Lara it's nice to meet you. Would you like a drink? How about a nice bottle of rosé?' asked Kel, as Patsy clapped her hands together in glee.

'Ah lovely Kel. Two glasses thanks Paddy,' Patsy said, smiling at Paddy behind the bar. Paddy grabbed an ice-bucket and filled it with ice, putting in a bottle of rosé and two glasses. Lara could see the trail of condensation that meandered down its silver surface.

'Usual Kel?' said Paddy, putting a cold corona with a slice of lemon in front of Kel. Kel gave him her card and he tapped it on the screen.

'Thanks mate,' said Paddy, as he motioned for the other bar person to come over. 'I'm clocking off Ted. Chelsea should be in around four.'

'No worries Paddy, enjoy your game of pool,' said Ted, continuing to polish the wine glasses.

'Read the board and weep suckers,' said a very competitive Janie, who had won the pool competition by three games.

Lara had taken her wine over to the nearest table and was watching a very enthusiastic Janie prance around the pool table. Who would have thought she was so competitive and so damn good at pool to boot? Curtis came over and joined her at the table.

'I bet you haven't witnessed this side of Janie before, hey Lara. She's a bit over the top when it comes to sports of any kind. Actually, that's probably why she's got such a great business, because she likes to be the best at whatever she does,' he said, taking a large sip of his beer.

'What about you Goldie, are you competitive like your sister?' she questioned, wanting to get to know him a bit more.

'Depends what I'm fighting for I guess. Pool, not so much, something I believe strongly in, well then yes, I want to win.'

'Well, what do you believe strongly in?' she asked, staring into his green eyes.

'The law for one. Family, love, freedom. What do you believe in Lara?'

'Oh well all of the above. Family, love—the right kind of love, not the bull dust one I was involved in. Let me see... Oh, definitely education. Education is the key to being able to get yourself out of poor situations like domestic violence and poverty. If you have a job that will support you then you can escape anything,' she said with conviction.

'Yeah, I agree, I've seen it in my job. But you know Lara, there are some people that are just victims and no amount of education will help them. My mum was a very educated woman, a doctor actually, a GP but nothing helped her...'.

'Hey Curtis come over here,' interrupted Kel, waving wildly to Curtis to come and take his turn at the pool table.

'Ah sorry Lara, I will finish this conversation another time, Kel looks like she's going to blow a gasket if I don't get over there quick enough.'

Damn it, thought Lara, as she realised she was about to get some more information about Curtis's childhood. She wanted to know everything about him. He was leaning on his pool stick watching Kel take a shot and she couldn't take her eyes off of him. His thick curly hair was haloed around his square jaw and his white t-shirt clung to his muscled chest. What she wouldn't give to rub her soft hands against the taunt material of his shirt. He started to laugh at something Kel and Paddy were saying. He had a gruff spontaneous laugh that made you stop and look.

'Hi Lara, this is my husband Brad,' said Tiffany, as she joined her at the table.

'Hello Tiff, glad you could make it. Hi Brad, nice to meet you,' she said, shaking the large man's hand and instantly seeing the resemblance between him and his two little daughters. By about 6pm it had turned into a real party. Finger foods of sour cream and chilli potato wedges, chicken wings, and margarita pizzas were ordered for everyone to share. Patsy was feeding coins into the jukebox next to the pool table and was playing all the hits. Lara loved all the stuff from the '70s and '80s: Cold Chisel, Eagles, Abba, definitely a bit of AC/DC but she also liked the latest pop songs by Taylor Swift or Ed Sheeran. Being an only child, she spent a lot of time with her mum and dad and they both loved to play their records on a Saturday afternoon. Lara loved watching them sing along with the artists. It was almost a competition between the two of them as to who knew all the words to the songs. They were both pretty good. When 'Dancing queen' came on the jukebox, all the girls got up to sing and dance. Lara was a bit shy about her dancing but couldn't resist getting up with her new friends and letting her hair down a bit. Her body swayed in time to the music and her dark brown hair moved softly from side to side; she closed her eyes and enjoyed listening to the lyrics.

When she opened her eyes she could see Curtis staring at her. With a startle she saw something in his green eyes and hoped it was in appreciation and not horror at the way she moved. When the next song came on, she begged off and went back to her table, grabbing a glass of water from the bar on the way. Best to knit one, pearl one she thought and then laughed to herself as she realised Pearl and Shirl were definitely rubbing off on her. Over by the other end of the bar Lara spied a group of about four guys all in leather jackets drinking beers. They had tatts and longish hair and some were sporting beards. *They look like scary guys,* she thought to herself as she turned back to find Paddy and Janie joining her. Chelsea, the bartender, came over with two more trays of food and put them down on the table to share. Lara thanked her and moved some of the glasses away to make room. Lara ordered another round of drinks and asked Chelsea to put it on her tab.

'Oh no don't look now but that looks like a few of the 'Wolf Pack' bikies, friends of the Olsen brothers,' said Paddy, taking a swig of his beer and pulling out a stool for Janie to sit on.

'Thanks, Paddy. I am not looking over there as I definitely don't want any trouble with them. Last time they came to town there was a kerfuffle down at the fruit grower's park. Too much alcohol and sun definitely doesn't gel,' replied Janie. She turned her head so that she could not see the bikies, grabbed a slice of pizza and called over the rest of the gang.

'Yeah great idea, I definitely don't want any trouble in here tonight. They seem pretty okay at the moment so let's just ignore them and have fun,' Paddy said smiling down at Janie. The rest of the group came over to the table to share the food. Lara was hoping to continue her conversation with Curtis, but it was too crowded and noisy in the busy pub.

'You know what guys, I might say my goodnight to you all. I have lots of schoolwork to do tomorrow and it's getting quite late.' Lara stood up and waved goodbye to everyone. They were in for the long haul by the looks of them as Tiff and Patsy begged her to stay for another dance, but she had destination syndrome and could think of nothing better than her home and bed.

On her way out the main door Curtis came up behind her and said, 'Do you mind if I walk you home? I don't like that the 'Wolf Pack' are back in town. They are real thugs and I don't feel comfortable with you walking alone.'

'Why thank you kind sir. If it makes you feel better, then by all means, I'd love it if you walked me home,' she laughed, as he pulled open the glass doors and let her walk through first. *What a gentleman,* she thought, smiling to herself.

As they walked past the beer garden Bart and Cameron Olsen were making their way towards the front door of the pub.

'Well, hello there, leaving already,' sneered Bart, as he stepped in front of them.

Lara felt an uneasy feeling grow in her stomach. *Why does this man creep me out so much?* she thought, being very grateful that Curtis had offered to walk her home.

'That's right Bart. I think some of your mates are in there so I wouldn't keep them waiting if I were you. Haven't seen you around in a while Cam?' he said, stepping around Bart and steering Lara to his left so that he was blocking her from Bart's leer.

'Yeah, I've been away on business, tying up loose ends in Melbourne. How are things going with you? A little birdie told me you'd come back to River Bend. How's that going for you?' he said, with a sly smile on his face.

'All good Cam. I've been here for a while now. But I was surprised to hear that you'd come home after living in the city for so long.'

'Well, we wanted to keep our father's legacy alive so it meant coming back to this damn one-horse town, at least until we work out what we are going to do,' he said, nodding at Lara and starting to walk toward the pub's front door.

Just as they were walking past Lara, Bart stopped and faced her saying, 'So how's that stray cat of yours going? Has it turned up *begging* at your front door or is it just the local cop hanging around?' Lara stared at him with her mouth agape not quiet believing he could be so rude, even in front of Curtis. She felt Curtis stiffen beside her and suddenly he took a giant step towards Bart and was standing chest to chest with the smaller man. Lara put her hand on his arm and gently steered him away. At that moment Cam stood in between the two men and turned Bart towards the pub door.

'Yeah, yeah come on Bart get going,' said Cam quickly, pushing his brother towards the pub in an effort to defuse the situation. 'See you around, Curtis.'

Curtis and Lara kept walking and Lara let out a sigh of relief knowing that the Olsen brothers had moved on.

'What a bloody dick,' said Curtis, between gritted teeth.

'You know these guys then?' she said, turning to Curtis in the hazy evening light.

'Yeah Lara, we all went to primary school together, River Bend Primary actually. They were a few years above me, but we all played footy together on the oval. Cam was a decent guy back then but Bart always had a chip on his shoulder. I haven't seen Cam since I left to go and live on the Mornington Peninsula. Then when I came back here to work, they were still living in the city. When their dad passed away last year and left them the feed and hardware store, they both came back to River Bend. Cam left just after that so this is the first time I've seen him.'

They reached the front steps of Lara's place and she turned to face him. The streetlight left a shadow on one side of his face, but she still managed to see something pass over his green eyes: regret, confusion, sadness, longing, she couldn't quite place which. She reached up to gently touch his cheek by instinct, as though his sadness was hurting her heart.

'Are you okay Curtis, you seem sad all of a sudden,' she whispered, as a barn owl hooted in the distance.

'I don't know Lara. I often wonder if I made the right decision coming back here. It's a place where everyone knows me and everyone knows my history. Sometimes I feel like there is no escaping our past in this town. No one forgets, everyone knows,' he said, in a solemn voice.

'Sometimes it can be better than people not knowing anything about you or not caring. I've only been here a short time, but I can see and feel how much you and Janie are loved and cared for by this town. I'd take that over indifference and solitude anytime. I'm not sure why you and Janie left in such a hurry and one day you might want to share that with me, but you've made a really good life here Goldie, just remember that. The big smoke's not all it's cracked up to be, believe me,' she said, cathartically as she realised how happy she was to be in this small Victorian country town. She could just make out his green eyes in the gloom of the streetlight and had a sudden urge to shift a wayward curl that was hanging over his brows out of the way so that she could see his expression. Was she reading this right, it felt like this could be the moment that they finally had their first kiss? But what if she was wrong and he only wanted friendship. She nearly reached up on her tippy toes to brush her lips against his just as the insistent blare of his mobile phone rang out breaking the magical moment.

He stepped back shaking his head as though to clear his thoughts and held his phone up to his ear. She could hear a tinny voice in the background.

'Yeah okay just a moment,' he said into the mouth piece and then held the phone to his chest.

'Sorry Lara I have to take this, it's a work thing. I'll see you tomorrow. Goodnight.' He turned around and walked back in the direction that they had come from.

Lara took the stairs slowly thinking about Curtis and what she had almost done.

God girl you probably dodged a bullet just then. She couldn't believe that she had nearly kissed him. If his phone had not gone off at that exact minute, she definitely would have and then what... How awkward would that have been living so close together and seeing each other nearly every day. She'd resolved to leave all thoughts of men and love behind her when she came all this way to live in River Bend and make this new start. No, she just had to push Curtis Gold from her mind, as far away as she could, because love was not on her agenda anymore, at least, for this new beginning.

14

Chapter Fourteen

Lara had made a nice routine for herself since she had been in River Bend. She would rise at 6am and go for a run through the town, to the park, and then an intensive twenty minutes up and down the dry riverbed. She would then turn around and run home, shower, and be at work by 8am. On one such morning she came across Marg taking an early morning stroll through the river path. Lara gave her quite the fright as she came up behind her and sang out, 'Good Morning.' Marg jumped and a look of terror swept over her features.

'Marg I'm so sorry I didn't mean to scare you. I feel terrible,' she said, as she pulled up beside Marg and touched her gently on the shoulder.

'Jeez I'm just a bit jumpy today, Lara, it's not your fault,' said Marg, holding her hand to her chest as if she was trying to massage her heart back into life.

'You were a thousand miles away. Is everything okay?' Lara asked.

'Well to be totally honest, it's the anniversary of my late husband's death. It was such a terrible day that I can't help reliving it in my mind.' She had a wobble in her voice and moist eyes.

Lara came to a complete stop and looked sadly at Marg, 'Gosh Marg, no wonder you were a million miles away. It's a very sad time for you, I'm sure.'

'It is. But you know, I have to get on with my life. It's been two years. I've learnt, not without its complications, to live without him. But he was the absolute love of my life and I miss him every day, especially on special occasions like birthdays and anniversaries.' Marg rested her hands over her heart.

'What are you doing tonight?' said Lara, with a hint of sympathy in her voice. She felt a bit of a shock that she was about to invite this lovely lady over to her house. 'Come for dinner and I'll get us a bottle of champagne and you can tell me all the special things about your husband.'

Marg's face lit up. 'Oh darling, that would be amazing. I had terrible thoughts about eating alone and wallowing in my sorrow.'

When Lara got home from work that night, she whipped together a butter chicken, filled the rice cooker with delicious jasmine rice, and set it to cook. Marg arrived at exactly 6pm, as if she had been waiting out the front for the minute hand to click over. She came with her arms full of champagne, chocolates, a delicious looking lemon tart, and a pot of whipped cream. Lara noticed that she had gone to a lot of trouble with her outfit; a nice pair of three-quarter length white jeans and a black lace short sleeved shirt. She wore a small amount of makeup and Lara thought that she now looked closer to her own age than her mother's, and that if she bothered to dye her hair, she would lose five years more.

It was still warm enough to enjoy their curry out on the balcony. They talked about Dave, Marg's husband, Zumba, country life, school, and social work. Sipping on the cold champagne they made a toast to Dave, and Marg told her some really lovely stories about their time together. Lara thought that it must be very cathartic for Marg to be telling an almost stranger funny and intimate parts of her marriage. Dave had been a farmer his whole life and had inherited the family farm from his dad when he was only twenty-one. His mother and father had been killed in a tragic car accident coming back from Melbourne on a cold and rainy winter night. Marg said the whole town mourned them. Dave was an only child, so he was left alone on the property.

'My first placement job as a social worker was at the community centre here in River Bend. I got to meet a lot of the farmers; the drought had really affected many of their mental health. Dave came in to have a chat and that was that, love at first sight,' she said, taking another bite of her lemon tart and scooping up some whipped cream.

'Wow Marg, love at first sight... That's so romantic. How did you know he was the right man for you?' Lara was really interested in her response.

'Hmmm, I don't know Lara,' Marg laughed. 'It was just a gut feeling. I remember I couldn't take my eyes off him and just wanted to spend more time with him. He asked me on a date and the rest was history. Thirty happy years of marriage. I was very young, only in my early twenties. My friends, of course, were sceptical about the wedding, but when they saw us together, they were so relieved to see how much in love we were.'

In her head Lara did the math; Marg was around fifty. 'So, you lived on the farm together for thirty something years. It must have been doubly hard for you to sell and then move to the township,' said Lara, trying to be discreet but really wanting Marg to keep talking about her life.

'Yes, one of the hardest decisions I think I have ever made, but I really had no choice. I couldn't take care of the farm on my own and I was so lonely. I just really needed to be around people that cared for me. Smithy was a real lifesaver at that time. He counselled me into making the right decision.'

'Smithy is such a lovely, caring man. I'm so glad you had his support.' Lara reached over and gave Marg's hand a squeeze.

'And what about you Lara, this has all been a one-sided conversation about me. Has Josh left town yet?' she asked, screwing up her eyebrows in concern.

'Aww that's the million dollar question. I have no idea and frankly as long as he stays away from me, I don't really care. I spent a lot of time worrying about Josh and I refuse to give him any more air space in my mind,' she let out a big sigh.

'Bravo to you Lara,' Marg said, raising her glass in a salute and continued, 'men should never have that power over us. I see it all the time in counselling and from what I gather he was not a very nice man to you, especially during Covid,' she queried.

'Correct Marg. He was abusive and it was a really horrible time for me. But look at me now, living and teaching in River Bend with so many new and lovely friends looking out for me,' she smiled warmly at Marg, not wanting the conversation to dwell on her time with Josh. She was over it.

'So many lovely new friends and may I ask about Curtis?' Marg laughed. 'Not wanting to be nosey but I sense a strong attraction between the two of you.'

'He's a lovely man but I've kind of sworn off love for a bit. I want to try and find my own feet, in my own time.' Lara's mind wandered to the very handsome Curtis Gold and the almost kiss.

'That's a wonderful idea Lara, find your own self and take things slowly. You never know what might happen in a country town. Love could be just around the corner,' she winked. 'Now come on, let's get these dishes done. I've had the nicest time lovely, and I really appreciate your friendship.' Marg got up and started clearing away the dirty dishes.

That night after Marg had left, Lara took a steamy cup of tea to her bed and opened up the book club book. Cosying in, she smiled to herself, *yes you never know what might happen in a sleepy country town. Love could be just around the corner or down the back stairs.*

$$15$$

Chapter Fifteen

'Lara, I was wondering if I could have a quick word with you after school?' Janie asked, one Wednesday morning when Lara had gone in to buy a salad roll for her lunch.

'Yeah of course Janie, is it anything I need to worry about? Eviction, noisy neighbour, bad choices in outfits!' Lara laughed and grabbed a breakfast muffin while she waited for her roll to be made up.

'It's matters of the heart, my friend,' Janie said whimsically. She added a layer of white mayonnaise to the top of the roll, wrapped it, and placed it in a brown paper bag.

Lara jumped in her car and headed towards school, her mind full of the activities she had planned for the day. There was a sports event happening in the afternoon that the senior students were running. Her little grade was excited to join and learn from the big kids.

When the home bell rang, Lara after being on the oval all afternoon in the summer heat, was tired and relieved to say goodbye to everyone. She quickly cleaned her desk and packed away the few loose crayons and papers that the children had accidentally left out. On her way home she started to think about what it was that Janie needed so desperately to talk about. When she got to her apartment she had a quick shower and changed into some comfortable leggings and a t-shirt and made her way down to the cafe. Janie was there cleaning up the last of the dishes. The delicious smell that hit Lara's nostrils made her mouth wa-

ter. She sniffed. *Cinnamon, apple, and maybe a touch of something else...
Ah, burnt sugar.*

'Hi there Lara come in, I won't be two seconds. Do you mind staying here, I just have to wait for the muffins to come out of the oven for tomorrow's breakfast?'

'Janie, this place smells like a dream. You are such an amazing cook, where did you learn it and is it catchy?' Lara replied, laughing at her own joke.

'My aunty was a chef; she was always in the kitchen baking something. I used to sit at the bench all the time and just watch her. Eventually she trusted me enough to start helping, and then I was making my own dishes. I love cooking. You measure, you follow a recipe, and you create. I don't understand why some people can't cook, Miss Lara,' she said laughing, and pulling a bottle of wine out of the industrial fridge.

'I'm not saying I *can't* cook, I'm saying I *don't* cook. There is a difference you know, Miss Smarty Pants. My mum hated cooking. She did the bare minimum and I think I just inherited that gene.'

'Anybody can cook Lara, you just have to want to. Now, come and sit over here and tell me what you think of this new Riesling that the 'Bend In The River' winery is producing down on Cliff Road. They've sent me a few bottles to try and I'm thinking of putting in an order for four cases. I hope you like it?' She poured a generous amount into Lara's beautiful hand painted wine glass.

'I wish I had your flair, Janie. You know how to dress, buy beautiful things, and run a busy business. I always feel like a frump around you,' sighed Lara, taking a sip of her cold Riesling.

'Stop it girl! You are amazing. You teach little kids for God's sake. I could never do that and you know, we all have our own style. You are the girl next door; wholesome, like Oliva Newton-John as Sandy in *Grease*, fit, an antipodean goddess jogging around the streets of River Bend. You are kind and sweet. Don't ever let anyone change you Lara Benton. You are you. And may I say I think my little brother has a crush as big as the bend in the river on your sweet little soul,' she said, with a knowing nod.

'Really? I think he's just being kind because I'm new in town,' Lara blushed.

'Not new anymore Lara. You have been here a couple of months now so the novelty of a new person should have worn off. No, he definitely has feelings for you. And I kind of think it might be reciprocated,' she smiled innocently.

'I have so sworn off men, Janie. After Josh I have definitely been burnt,' she said, with a determined shake of her head.

'So, you are telling me that you feel nothing for Curtis?' she said, surprised. 'I don't know how my radar got that so wrong. I am normally one hundred percent right in my predictions of love. That hug I witnessed in the beer garden was just two friends having an intimate moment then. Okay, I'll just have to go back to the drawing board.'

'Well talking about love, what's going on with you and Paddy?' asked Lara, trying to turn the conversation away from her and her non-existent love life.

'I don't know, we are always so busy. That's kind of what I wanted to talk to you about. I need a girlfriend's ear,' she sounded desperate. Lara felt quite chuffed to be considered as one of Janie's girlfriends.

'We are both working such long hours, and he works most nights. I just don't know how we could ever make anything work at this rate,' she shook her head sadly.

'Come on Janie, if you like the guy, and I'm pretty sure you do—ha that's my love radar going off the charts, then you have to try and make time. You just have to my friend,' said Lara, with a determination in her tone.

'I know you're right, but what do I do? I can't just ask him out. I'd die of embarrassment if he said no and never be able to have another drink in the Rivy Arms as long as I live. Now that would be a disaster.' Janie shook her head slowly and pursed her lips.

'Okay I can see how awkward that would be, but there must be a way that you two can get together. What are your famous love vibes telling you about Paddy and you, seeing you are so good at picking couples,' she said, with a wink?

'I think he likes me Lara, but I don't want to ruin what we already have. What happens if I ask him out and he says no? I'd just die.' She reached for the bottle and refilled their glasses.

'Well, okay I get that, but does it have to be a date as such?' said Lara, making air quotes in the sky when she said the word date. 'Why don't we organise a dinner party? You know, we could say something like you are teaching me to cook and I need a guinea pig or something like that.' Lara felt very positive about her plan.

'We'd have to ask someone else. It would look a bit suss if it was just the three of us. Maybe we could invite Curtis along and some of the other crew.' Janie seemed to like the idea of a dinner party.

'Hang on, if I'm cooking for the first time, I am definitely not cooking for half the town! How about I speak to Curtis and see what he says, and then get him to ask Paddy? That way, you don't have anything to do with the guest list,' said Lara, taking another sip of her drink. 'This is really yummy wine Janie. I think you should definitely order some. Now let's get back to business. What on earth am I going to cook at this dinner party?'

$$16$$

Chapter Sixteen

Tiffany answered the door holding a tray of champagne glasses. 'Here Lara have some bubbles, not only is it my first book club but we are celebrating my new home,' Tiffany said, with the widest smile on her face, handing Lara a cold champagne glass full of bubbling liquid as she walked into the lounge.

'I'll have one of those thanks pet,' smiled Shirl, reaching to take a glass from the tray Tiff held.

'Your home is lovely pet. You know this property used to belong to the Fitzgerald's who left after the last drought and were never sighted again. Apparently, they went to live in the city. Couldn't take the country life. It's hard yakka on the land. It takes a certain type you know. Any who,' said Pearl, finally stopping to take a breath and a small sip of her champagne.

Tiffany had certainly turned the old cottage into a lovely home. She had gone op-shopping in Talbot and bought an old comfy couch that she still couldn't believe someone was silly enough to give away rather than sell on Marketplace. 'I love all the new slash old things you have bought Tiff. Marketplace must be your new best friend,' said Patsy.

'It sure is I got the girls' beds and dressing table from there, as well as, that beautiful old art deco dining table and chairs.' Tiffany pulled out one of the orange chairs to show the ladies as they all nodded their heads in approval at her purchase. 'And Lara and I had the best time shopping in Adelaide last weekend. I bought colourful throws with matching yellow sunflower doona covers for the girls.'

Lara looked over at Marg while the rest of the crew picked fruit and cheese before the book club officially started and smiled, 'How's things with you Marg?'

'Okay thanks Lara, I was hoping you and I could have another chat sometime soon,' she said, with a sigh.

'I'm free tomorrow, why don't you call in for dinner after work?' Lara had developed quite a warm relationship with Marg over the few months she had been in River Bend. Marg felt almost like a mother figure or older sister to her than a normal friendship, like she had with Janie, Tiffany and Patsy.

'Please, you must come to my place tomorrow Lara, after you've worked all day, I'd love to cook for you.' The smile came back onto Marg's face at the thought of looking after someone. Her eyes shone as if she were going through favourite recipes in her mind.

'So, we all agree then this was a little ripper of a book and oh what a love story! That Ari was a bit of alright too, he can put his hush puppies under my bed anytime,' Shirl laughed, picked up her drink and took another sip.

'Well Shirley Early, you old dog,' laughed Patsy, turning to a page in her book and perusing it.

'I'm not dead yet Patsy. An old lady can dream, can't she?' Shirl reached over and took a small wedge of cheese and quince paste and popped it into her mouth, smiling warmly at her friend.

The ladies spent a good hour and a half discussing the ins and outs of their book club book. Travel, war, unrequited love, true love, betrayal, this book had it all and led to some interesting discussion. 'I just loved *I remember you*, that opening prologue left me in tears.' Historical Romance is my new favourite genre. So, what's our next book?' asked Lara, after they had finished discussing the novel.

'A friend of mine recommended a book, I just can't think of its name but it's about forced adoption in the '70s and '80s,' said Janie, scrolling through her phone looking for the name of the book.

'Wow that sounds pretty interesting, hurry up and find the title so I can google it,' said Patsy, grabbing her phone.

Lara heard a gasp come from Marg's lips as she looked at her friend who had gone a pale white.

'Marg, are you okay? Here, have some water.' Lara poured her a glass of ice water from a jug on the coffee table. Marg took the water with a thankful look. Her hand shook slightly as she took a gulp of the cooling drink.

'I'm sorry ladies, my biscuit went down the wrong way,' she said, putting down the glass with a shaky hand and coughing into her tissue.

'Oh no, are you all right Marg, can I get you anything?' asked a concerned Tiffany.

'No, I'm all good thanks Tiff. I might head off, its way past my bedtime,' Marg said, getting up from the chair and grabbing her handbag. 'Thanks for a lovely evening, Tiffany. I thoroughly enjoyed it. Please let me know what the next book is,' she said, walking towards the front door. As a good hostess Tiffany followed Marg to the door and made sure she got into her car safely.

Strange, thought Lara, *what was all that about? Hopefully I'll find out tomorrow.*

Nobody else in the room seemed to notice Marg's discomfort so Lara let it go. The book club went on for another half an hour with everyone trying to talk over each other as they discussed other things apart from the book. The talk turned to Smithy and how he was left a widower five years ago when his wife was diagnosed with breast cancer. 'That's just so sad. He is such a lovely man,' said Lara, feeling terribly sorry for the man who always asked how she was, and how she had settled into life at River Bend.

'Fair dinkum, she was such a lovely lady. Honestly, it hit the town hard when she passed away. Old Smithy just kept on going. As the only

GP in our town he knew he was needed,' Pearl said, as she got up and carried the near empty platter into the kitchen. When she re-entered she grabbed her handbag and said, 'Well thanks pet for a lovely night but I think it's time Shirl and I hit the frog and toad,' she headed towards the door.

Lara followed and gave Tiffany a quick hug thanking her for a wonderful night. Janie and Lara walked home in the cool evening enjoying the way the stars played in the night sky, with the full moon illuminating their path. Janie linked arms with her friend and said, 'Well Lara, out of ten, how was your first book club experience?'

'Loved it Janie, ten out of ten. I just feel so happy that I am fitting into this little town. It was a good decision to come to River Bend, that's for sure.'

Lara's Research:
Fair dinkum: honestly, really
Hit the frog and toad: hit the road, leave.

17

Chapter Seventeen

Janie helped Lara select a pecan pie from the fridge to take to Marg's house that night. It looked delicious and smelled even better. She had also grabbed a local Shiraz from the IGA that afternoon to go with the fruity taste of the pie. As she walked up Main Street towards Marg's house she couldn't help worrying about her new friend. Lara knew that she was lonely and missing her late husband, but it seemed even more than that. She had a gut feeling that Marg had something else on her chest that she wanted to let go of tonight. The flowering gum trees had lost their beautiful red buds due to the change in season, but they still looked majestic and strong guarding the side walk. It left her with such an overwhelming sense of wellbeing that she stopped in her tracks and held her heart as it beat in her chest. *How lucky am I?* she thought as she reflected on her new life and how at ease she felt in the town. She walked past the Cut & Shine and waved to Patsy through the window. She looked like she was cutting the hair of a small boy and had a determined look of concentration on her face. From where she was standing, she could hear the shrieks of the small child, crying out in torment at being subjected to having his hair cut off. Lara couldn't imagine having a child, especially having to go through milestones like first haircuts, toilet training, and first day at school. When she was with Josh she had dreamed of having her own family, but as their relationship deteriorated she was so glad that she had kept on the pill and not been manipulated by him into getting pregnant. All Josh talked about was starting a family. When she looked back on their relationship, Lara shuddered at the thought of bringing an innocent baby into that toxic situation. Thank the Gods she had never relented on that one thing. If Josh had found her pills, he would have been furious at her deceit; it probably would have ended in a beating. But birth control was something she felt she must challenge him on, even if she did it without his knowledge, because poor doormat Lara wasn't capable of challenging him. She just kept it a secret, just like she kept her toxic relationship a secret from her parents until that one night where it all went to hell in a handbasket.

As she approached Marg's home, she couldn't help admiring the gorgeous cottage garden out the front. One day Lara would like to live in a cottage like Marg's. Maybe she would eventually have kids if she found the right life partner. That made her mind travel to Goldie, and she couldn't help wondering if she was being silly and selfish not trying to build a relationship with him. She thought that he liked her; he was always attentive and caring when he was around her. But then so was Josh at the beginning. *No, silly, Goldie is nothing like Josh,* she said to herself for the hundredth time. She felt like she was building up a wall between them that had absolutely nothing to do with him or how she felt, it was just a gut reaction left over from stupid Josh and the hurt she still carried. Could she and Curtis live in a house like this one day? Could they raise a family together? Could they be kind and caring towards each other? Could she love him unreservedly and, more to the point, could he love her with kindness, compassion and, most importantly, respect. She thought that perhaps they could build a life together if only she could discard the trauma of her past.

She stood on the porch and admired the beautiful lead light windowpane depicting a scene of cockatoos and sparrows on an old gum tree. It was so full of tiny details and when she looked even closer, she could see the twisting limbs of the gum and the black claws of the cockatoos resting on its branches. While she was looking, the door opened and Marg stood there in a gingham apron with a small sandy terrier sniffing at her feet. When the door fully opened the little dog started barking at the stranger standing in the doorway.

'Be quiet Missy, you will scare our guest off. Hello Lara, come in and don't be frightened of her. Her bark is worse than her bite,' laughed Marg, swiping up Missy from the floor and gently smoothing down the soft hair on her head.

'Well hello there young Missy, you certainly have a loud bark for such a little dog.' Lara reached out her hand in a fist for Missy to sniff. Suddenly a small pink tongue came out and licked the back of her hand. Lara laughed at the feel of the sandpaper tongue roughly tickling her skin. 'She's adorable Marg. Can I have a hold?' asked Lara, reaching out for the little dog.

'Yes of course you can love. She's such a little smooch. Now come in and let's get you a drink.'

Lara walked down the long corridor and couldn't help looking at the beautiful ornate chandeliers that hung from the high ceilings. The ceiling roses were painted in a sage green colour and the roof and walls were a deep cream. The floorboards were stained a dark wood that contrasted beautifully with the walls. Artwork depicting the local area adorned both sides of the hallway. Lara stopped at one and Marg said, 'That's a painting by a local artist showing the bend in the river the town is named after.'

'Curtis showed me that exact site at the Australia Day picnic, but of course it is bone dry now not like this. I can't believe that the river can flow so high,' she said in wonder.

'The saying goes you are not a real local until you see the bend in the river flow at least three times,' laughed Marg, heading off towards a door at the end of the hallway.

As Marg opened the heritage looking door a delicious smell wafted into the space. Lara walked into a big country style kitchen and lounge room. The kitchen had large black granite counters and inlaid wooden doors and drawers the same colour as the floorboards in the hallway. Glass pendants hung from the roof over the benches on wrought iron chains, and there was a huge stainless-steel oven and white enamel sink taking up one whole side of the room with a picture window overlooking a green field. From beyond the kitchen, Lara could see a lounge room that opened up onto a covered veranda. It was the most stunning room she had ever seen and for some reason it surprised her that Marg lived in such a beautiful, tasteful home. Why that was she would have to analyse later but when she thought about it, everything about Marg was tasteful; her sense of dress, well except for Zumba class, the way she carried herself around the town, and the respect she was given by everyone that knew her.

'Here Lara, try this.' Marg passed Lara a glass full of a vibrant green coloured liquid. 'It's my famous Japanese Slipper.'

'Yum what's in it?'

'Let me see Midori, Cointreau and lemon. Cheers.'

Lara tasted the cold liquid and felt the sweetness dance on her tongue. 'Marg this is divine. How have I never had this cocktail before? And me a city girl,' laughed Lara. She sat on one of the recycled stools that stood next to the bench where Marg was preparing the drinks. Missy had gone back to her comfortable looking bed that was placed near the brown leather rocker in front of a giant TV screen.

'Something smells delicious Marg. What have you been cooking up?'

'It's my auntie's shepherd's pie recipe. It's so tasty and I wanted to have something prepared so that I didn't waste time in the kitchen.'

'That sounds like it could work for my dinner on Saturday night. I've got Janie and Paddy and Curtis coming over for my very first dinner party. I've been getting a few tips from Janie.'

'That sounds very interesting, you have to elaborate. I'm happy to share Aunt Pauline's recipe with you, and if you like I can even come over after Zumba and help you get it ready. Only if I'm not encroaching of course.'

'Are you serious? That would be amazing. Poor Janie was going to help me but she has just got a huge booking for Saturday lunch from that new winery, Bend In The River.' Lara felt relief descend over her as she realised she wouldn't have to cancel the dinner party after all if Marg was going to help her.

'I would love to help. Before you go, and of course if you like the shepherd's pie, I will write out a shopping list. You can get everything from the IGA in town.'

'You are a lifesaver Marg.'

Marg and Lara had a lovely evening together enjoying the tasty pie and talking about the local town gossip.

'So that was how Pearl and Shirl ended up working at the IGA after being retired for nearly a decade,' finished Marg, piling the dishes into the dishwasher.

They took their coffees out onto the veranda where Missy sniffed in the lantana looking for rabbits or old forgotten bones. She kept looking up to make sure Marg was still within eyesight.

'Poor little Missy is a bit shy about coming out in the back garden on her own after she had the run in with the snowdropper a few months ago,' said Marg, settling into her wicker chair.

'That's right, I remember the night you came into the pub. How horrible, I didn't realise that you had been home when the snowdropper hit. I know how awful I felt when that guy was peeping through my window. It leaves you feeling so vulnerable.' Lara felt another level of sadness for her friend.

'I'm so lucky,' Marg said. 'Curtis came over the next day and set up extra locks and a camera, and he even got his mate to install sensor lights all around my property. It took Missy a while to get used to the lights going on and off when she would go out for her toileting.' She picked up her coffee and took a sip.

Lara couldn't help but feel gratitude for Curtis and all that he does for his friends and the town. 'Marg, I got the sense that you had something on your mind that you wanted to discuss with me.' Lara nibbled at her bottom lip nervously. She didn't want to put any pressure on Marg to confide in her, but she sensed that Marg might need a gentle push.

'Yes, you are quite right Lara. It's just hard to know where to start. The only person who knows is Dave and he can't really help me now,' she shook her head sadly.

'In my experience Marg, sometimes you just have to start at the beginning and see where that takes you.' A barn owl hooted softly in the background and Missy lifted up her little head to sniff the night air. When it stopped she went back to sniffing the ground around the bushes and dug her nose into the soft dirt.

'Okay well here goes, when I was a young girl, sixteen to be exact, I had a baby. There I said it.' Marg put her hand up to her necklace and started playing with the gold heart attached to it.

'Marg you were so young, what happened to the baby?' Lara blurted out before she could stop herself.

'Yes, I was very young. Too young to raise a child or so my strict catholic parents thought. They sent me off to a convent near Ballarat, "The Holy Redeemer". I spent six months there and when it was time to have the baby, oh Lara, it was awful. The nuns didn't give me any pain relief and when the baby finally came out they just whisked it away and I never got to see its sweet little face,' Marg said, crying into her tissue.

'Oh God Marg, that is so sad. How horrible!'

'The worst part was that the placenta got stuck and they left some of it in there to rot in my uterus. When the infection got so bad I had to have an emergency hysterectomy and that's why I can't have children. My parents said it was God's way of making sure I never strayed again. When I turned eighteen, I left my family home and haven't been back or seen my parents since. My aunty wrote to tell me that my dad passed away just one year after I left. He died of liver cancer and then my mum apparently died the next month. They say she died of a broken heart but honestly Lara as far as I'm concerned, she didn't have a heart. I know that sounds cruel but it's the truth. They would never even tell me if it was a boy or girl. Since Dave's death I've been thinking a lot about the baby. It would be in its mid-thirties now. How could the nuns be so cruel?' she continued to weep into her sodden tissue.

Lara reached out and rubbed her friend's back, trying to console her. 'What a terrible time it was back then for unwed mothers, Marg. Honestly, I feel so powerless for you,' she continued to rub her back in small circles. 'Have you ever thought about trying to find your child? I know there are organizations that can help in situations like this,' asked Lara.

'Oh love, I could never do that. I'm just not ready to take that step yet. What happens if the child resents me, or if they have had a terrible life? I think I would die. Over the years I've built an imaginary bubble of my baby living with a loving couple who've made the most wonderful family, I don't want to burst that. It's just so nice to finally have someone else who knows my darkest secret.'

'It's not a sinister, dark secret. It's a tragedy that you and many young girls during that time had to endure. When you are ready to find your child Marg, if you are ever ready, I'm here for you,' Lara said, with conviction.

18

Chapter Eighteen

Curtis single-handedly carried the trestle table out of his back shed. 'Where did you want to set this up, Lara?' he asked.

'I was thinking, as it's such a nice night, we could have dinner out on the veranda. I've also bought some fairy lights to hang up if you have time to help me,' said Lara. She returned to mashing the potato for the shepherd's pie. Marg had helped her make the base and had just left after giving her strict instructions on what ingredients to add and when to add them. Lara was starting to feel quite confident that the food for her dinner party was going to be at least edible, maybe even delicious if it turned out anything like the pie she had at Marg's the other night. Thinking about Marg and her baby made Lara feel sad so she forced herself to brush it aside for now. There was just too much to do.

'I'll just run down and grab my step ladder, Lara. I won't be a minute.' Curtis ran down the steps to go and fetch his equipment. From her position on the balcony Lara could see Janie's guests starting to leave the cafe. *That's good,* she thought. Janie would have plenty of time to clean up and get ready for the date, well secret date, since Paddy had no idea the dinner party was really a ploy to get him and Janie together.

After she had set up outside and was happy with the arrangement of the table, the beautiful gold place mats she'd purchased online from Kmart looked stunning and a centrepiece of roses gave the table a pop of colour, Lara went to get ready. Before she jumped in the shower, she did a quick check on her progress so far. *Table setting done, cheese board on the bench, champagne and beer on ice, shepherd's pie ready to put in the oven, and one of Janie's delicious plum and rhubarb pies and cream in the fridge.*

When she had showered, she blow waved her hair straight and put on a sweet little brown Alice band that held her thick hair off her face. She had also purchased a new dress for the occasion. There was only one clothes shop in the whole of River Bend and it really only sold jeans, shorts, t-shirts and windcheaters so she had gone into Talbot last weekend with Janie. They had a boutique there that sold some really trendy outfits. She bought a pink and white gingham maxi dress that suited her tall frame perfectly. On her feet she slipped on some brown leather sandals. Lara was pleased with what she saw in the mirror and gave a little twirl. She put on some lip gloss, and to make her blue eyes pop, she applied a coat of mascara. For some reason she was feeling really excited about giving her very first dinner party. It made her feel grown up all of a sudden. Josh had never let her have anyone at the house, mind you, with lockdown it was kind of impossible to entertain like this. It annoyed her that at any given moment Josh could pop into her mind and take up space. She was beginning to understand the power and hold he had had over her during that time and was especially relieved to realise that he was out of her life.

Lara sat out on the veranda enjoying the beginning of Autumn with Janie and Curtis who had arrived bearing chocolates and wine. Curtis even produced a beautiful bunch of freesias from his garden for her. His dark curls looked damp from his shower, and Lara could smell the pine shampoo he favoured when he reached past her to grab a biscuit and cheese, his arm brushed against hers, their skin-to-skin contact sending a shiver down her back bone. He looked particularly handsome in a navy and white striped shirt and denim jeans. The cotton material pulled taught around his large biceps making her want to rub her hand up and down his arms to feel the bulge of his muscles under her soft fingers.

Lara diverted her attention to the space she had created and felt proud of its beauty. The fairy lights were the perfect touch to make the area look inviting. Paddy arrived not long after dressed in a white, short sleeve shirt and chinos; he looked like he had gone to a lot of trouble with his outfit. He brought a bottle of Aperol Spritz for them all to try. Lara went to get them glasses and ice for Paddy to pour the drinks. He started with prosecco, added the Aperol Spritz, and then, pulling out a snap lock bag, he added a slice of orange to each glass. It was a pretty orange colour and tasted delicious if not a little bitter. He said it was all the rage in Italy and that when he was in Lucca, he would drink it all the time. Lara had been there on her Contiki tour when she went to Florence. Suddenly she remembered she had wanted to ask Curtis if he had ever travelled.

'So, Curtis, Janie have you two ever travelled or been overseas?' she asked the two of them, taking a small sip of her delicious drink.

'I've only ever been to Queensland with my aunty when I was in high school,' said Janie. 'I've always imagined travelling the world but with the cafe and my life here, there just never seems time. Curtis did a lot of travel before the police academy...'

Her brother picked up the conversation, 'I took a couple of gap years after school and headed up north to Alice Spring where I got work on one of the big outstations as a jackaroo. God it was a rugged country, so different to this.' Curtis fanned out his hands to encompass the orange and green trees that grew along the nature strip below the veranda. 'I would go out for days at a time chasing the cattle, just throwing a swag under a tree and looking at the big expanse of sky.' He wore a wistful expression as though he were seeing it all laid out in front of him. *Sounds like he loved it,* thought Lara, looking intently at his eyes as they crinkled with his thoughts. 'I then headed to Darwin and worked in a bottle shop and lived in a caravan park. Bloody interesting job that was. I only lasted a few weeks and then handed in my notice and headed across to Broome, where I worked on a tourist boat taking punters out to the Kimberley region. It was absolutely breathtaking scenery but the demands of the rich and famous were definitely not for me. So, from there I jumped on a flight to Indonesia where I bought a motorbike and travelled through Southeast Asia living on the smell of an oily rag. I ended up in 4000 Islands, Laos, as remote a place as you can be, and taught English to the local children.'

By this time Lara's mouth was open and shutting as if she could not believe the sensible, well-respected policeman sitting in front of her had had such an interesting life. Here she was thinking her whirlwind trip through Europe on her safe and predictable Contiki was the bee's knees of adventure. She honestly had thought that Curtis had grown up in River Bend, moved to Melbourne, joined the police academy, and had come back to River Bend, end of story.

'Lara, you would have loved the little kids on 4000 Islands. I remember one day taking a group of them to one of the most beautiful waterfalls I had ever seen, nearly on a par with Henderson's Lookout Janie, and they were like little cormorants diving into the water, going deep down and spluttering back up. I was beside myself with panic as they all just, one, two, three jumped into the water. I thought they were all going to drown on me, until I realised they were all better swimmers than me, and I grew up on the back beaches of the Mornington Peninsula like Gunnamatta and Smiths Beach,' he laughed, reminiscing on what sounded like a crazy day.

'Curtis you sneaky old dog, I never knew you had such an interesting and varied life before becoming a policeman. I am super jealous and where is this Henderson's Lookout? Is that another exotic place you have been to?' laughed Lara, realising that she hadn't really seen that much of the world.

'Come on Lara, ten countries in Europe isn't anything to sneeze at. Henderson's Lookout is about five hours from here and one of the most beautiful places I have ever seen. It borders Victoria and South Australia. I'm going near there next weekend if anyone's up for a road trip and swag night,' he gave Lara a soft pat on the arm which sent a trillion shivers down her spine.

'I'd love that Curtis. Janie, Paddy can you come?' she asked, turning to face them.

'Oh bugger, Ted's got a buck's night so I have to work, maybe next time,' answered Paddy.

'I think I should be okay. I'll just have to check if one of the Early twins will look after the cafe,' said Janie, turning towards Lara and giving her a sweet smile. 'But you do realise I'm feeling like the loser in this group, I've been nowhere.'

'Hey at least you've been to Henderson's Lookout,' said Paddy, 'I am definitely taking a rain check on that camping trip.'

'And Janie, look at what you have created in this small country town. A wonderful place, and there's plenty of time for travel to be sure,' Curtis said, in a mock Irish brogue.

'Yes, maybe one day I'll get to your Emerald Isle, Paddy and I'll walk those Cliffs of Moher,' she said, with a longing in her expression.

'I'd love to show you my hometown lass, you would love the pubs there. The musicians just play all night sitting at a little table while people drink Guinness and do an Irish jig.'

The pie was an outstanding success. Paddy even joked about adding it to his Parma list as in 'Shepherd's pie Parma.' Lara got up from the table and asked Curtis to help her organise dessert. He followed her into the kitchen carrying some of the dirty dishes.

'Wow, I think this secret date is going really well, Curtis. He must like her if he is talking about taking her to his home village,' whispered Lara into his ear.

'Little Miss Matchmaker you,' laughed Curtis, starting to put the dirty dishes into the dishwasher.

'I'm just going to whip the cream but stay in here with me and help dish out the plum and rhubarb pie if that's okay. I want to give them a bit of privacy. Can you see what's going on?' she said, turning her head trying to look out the window as she whipped up the cream.

'Goodness me Lara Benton you are a little matchmaker,' and with that he reached over and scooped out a small dollop of cream and wiped it on her nose. She opened her mouth like a goldfish not quite knowing what to do.

'Did you just put cream on my nose?' she said, side eyeing him as she took a finger full of whipped cream and smeared it on his cheek.

'You are not starting a food fight surely. You are the mature teacher of little children who has travelled Europe on a bus full of mature people.' He gently grabbed her hands between their bodies and bending down licked the cream off her nose with his tongue.

She felt the skin tingle where his tongue had been a second ago. It was about the sexiest thing Lara had ever experienced and a gasp escaped from her mouth before she had time to stop it. Slowly, he turned his head and released one of her hands. He pointed to the cream on his cheek as if expecting her to reciprocate. He was so close that she could smell the orange from the Aperol Spritz on his breath. She stood up on her tippy toes and leant her head in towards his cheek, shyly poked out her tongue and in one swoop took the cream, balancing it on the tip before slowly swallowing. She left a tiny smear behind. Her heart was pounding in her chest and a thousand tiny butterflies were bouncing around her stomach. She had never felt so out of her depth sexually before. It was such a foreign feeling for her to be doing what she was doing, honestly licking cream from his cheek. She blushed as she felt the warmth of his body so close. If he moved his head an inch their lips would touch. In a husky voice she said softly, 'What's happening here Curtis?'

He replied into the soft strands of her hair, 'Whatever you would like to happen, Lara.' From the doorway behind her she heard somebody clearing their throat as a warning they were no longer alone.

'Ah sorry guys, I'm just bringing in the rest of the dishes,' Janie laughed at catching them out.

They jumped apart as if an electric shock had gone off between them. 'Oh no it's fine Janie. Curtis just got some whipped cream on his face and I was wiping it off,' Lara stammered and turned towards the bowl, picking up the beaters to give the cream a good mixing.

'To be sure to be sure,' laughed Janie in an Irish brogue while placing the dirty dishes on the bench top and giving her brother the once over.

'I kind of think this is the second time I've caught you two mucking around, maybe this dinner party is more for you than it is for me.' With that she turned and walked back out onto the veranda with a huge smile on her face.

'Okay dessert time, are you ready?' Lara said to Curtis, trying to hide her embarrassment at being the subject of Janie's amusement. She felt like a child getting caught with her hand in the lolly jar.

'Ready as ever,' said Curtis, holding two bowls of plum pie and cream, heading outside to the others. Lara stared after him and just couldn't shake the feeling of his hot tongue on the tip of her nose.

How embarrassing, she thought, *get a grip girl or you are going to fall really hard for this guy, and guys are just not your thing at the moment.* She headed out to the others with a bowl of pie in each hand and tried to block the thought of Curtis Gold and his powerful presence from her mind.

19

Chapter Nineteen

Lara was meeting Curtis at the Rivy Arms to organise their upcoming trip to Henderson's Lookout. 'I'm so glad you have invited me away next weekend Curtis but what a shame Janie can't make it. If you want to cancel...' Lara handed over her card to shout her round of drinks for their planning session.

'Yeah, it was such a last-minute thing for Janie to realise she had a booking at the cafe too big for the Early's to handle. I have to go anyway as I need to call into one of the stations out there to drop off some paperwork and take some photos for an insurance job, but if you don't want to come, I completely understand.' He took their drinks over to the table.

'Oh no I am super keen to see Henderson's Lookout, and the weather forecast is fantastic for the weekend. As long as you don't mind just my company,' she got out her notebook.

'What's that for?' he asked with a smile.

'I don't want to forget anything, and you know I like to be organised so hit me with a list of things we will need.'

On Friday after work Curtis met her in her classroom and helped her carry all the things she had packed, out to his car.

'I am so looking forward to sleeping in a swag. This is going to be so much fun.' Lara had borrowed the swag from Patsy.

They took off towards Charlotte's Bridge with the sounds of 3KK easy listening music, playing on the radio. The countryside changed from the green of cattle country to the red dirt of the wheat growing lands. Trees became sparse and small green and brown bushes dotted the landscape with the occasional kangaroo jumping alongside them. Lara was glad it was Curtis driving as she remembered her last run in with a roo. Dusk was not a good time to be on the roads in country Victoria; the kangaroos had a habit of just jumping out in front of cars.

Luckily they made it to the free camp without mishap and set up for the night. The campsite had a solar powered kitchen and soon Curtis had the sausages sizzling on the grill. They sat around on their foldout chairs eating sausages and fried potatoes while the sun sank in the west and put a majestic glow over everything. The weather was perfect for sitting around at dusk and even though they didn't really need it, Curtis made a small fire in the fire pit. It added to the atmosphere of camping and Lara loved it. He had even thought of bringing marshmallows which they had fun toasting.

'It's so peaceful here Goldie,' Lara said, as an owl of some description hooted in the background. 'This is what I missed during lockdown and city life. Just looking up at this amazing night sky and seeing all the stars. It's heaven.' She put her head back on the head rest of her camp chair and stared up at the map of sparkling stars above her. In a blaze of light, a falling star streaked through the other bright stars and disappeared into the darkness. Lara held her breath and made a wish. 'Was it fun growing up around here?' she asked, forgetting that he had really only been here as a child.

'Well, I left when I was six but did come back for school holidays and stayed at Smithy's, I was good friends, am good friends, with his youngest son Peter. Smithy was great; he would always take us kids camping and show us the ropes. Like how to build a fire or how to catch a fish. They were a great support to me and Janie when we were younger. My mum worked with him for a bit before she got pregnant with me.'

'Yes that's right, I remember you telling me that your mum was a G.P., but I didn't realise she worked in River Bend?'

'It was just for a short time, my father needed her to help on the farm. We grew up out west, about an hour from River Bend, and Dad said that two hours travelling a day was a waste of time. Besides, he needed her. Or so he said...' A shadow passed across Curtis's eyes and he scratched his chin as if deep in thought. 'It's difficult for me to go back to that time, I have pretty terrible memories of growing up. My father was a violent man. It's hard for me to say it out loud, but he was just plain mean. I hated him, Lara. There were times when Janie and I would hide in the cupboard listening to the abuse he would inflict on our mother and we would just hold each other for comfort, always scared that he was going to come and have a go at us. Even to this day I feel guilty that I did nothing to stop him from hurting my mum.'

'God Goldie you were just a child.' Lara reached over and placed her hand gently on his knee.

'Yeah well, I still feel like shit about it all. Anyway, one day my Mum had had enough and got one of the rifles out of the gun cupboard and shot him in the head.'

'Jesus Curtis,' she said, putting her hand up to her mouth in shock.

'She made sure that Janie and I were at school so we actually don't know what happened for sure. My aunty came up and collected us from the police station and we never saw Mum again. Apparently, she ended up in a high security mental institution in New South Wales and refused any visitors. When I was older, I wrote to her for a while but never got a reply so I guess I just gave up trying. My aunty never told us much except that Mum was sick and didn't want to see anyone.'

'Oh Goldie, I am so sorry that you had to go through all that, especially at such a young age.' Tears formed at the corners of her eyes.

'Thanks, Lars. We have learnt to live with our past and I honestly think it has made me a stronger, better person. I was always scared that some of my father's genes may have rubbed off on me, but I realised Janie and I are nothing like him and never will be. I feel so sorry for my mum because I know she sacrificed herself for us. I can still remember what she went through, and it was bloody awful,' he lowered his head into his hands.

Lara knelt down in front of him and took his hands gently in her own and pulled them down to look deep into his eyes. 'I don't know you that well yet but what I do know is that you are a kind and gentle person. So don't you ever believe you are anything like your father. You are not, you are a wonderful human being.' She stared into his deep green eyes and cupped the side of his face so that he would not lose her stare. As if on auto pilot she moved towards him and their lips touched, firing up every nerve in her body. It was like nothing she had ever experienced before. An overwhelming feeling of tenderness and love enveloped her whole body. Her lips parted with his as he gently moved his mouth to fit hers. She felt the warmth of his arms fold around her, bringing her closer to him as if he were drowning and she was his life raft. Somehow, she ended up on his knee and that first touch of lips on lips became a deeper, more passionate kiss. Lara never wanted it to end, she felt her heart beating as fast as it did when she'd just run the river bend. Her hands moved through his hair, getting tangled in the thick curls. Her breath became ragged and a small moan escaped her. When they finally came up for air she nestled her head against his chest and held him. He gently stroked her hair. Lara couldn't believe the overwhelming feeling of tenderness that she felt for him at that very moment. The sound of possums fighting in the tree beside them shook them out of their position and she slowly got off his knee and took her own seat again.

'Thanks Lara, I really appreciate you listening to me. I hope you are not turned off knowing my family secret. It's not something I tell a lot of people but opening up to you feels right; therapeutic in a way. I just can't explain it,' his voice raspy, he shook his head and took her hand in his.

It felt right to be sitting in the dark bush of country Victoria, just silently holding hands and gaining strength from each other. Lara turned her head to look at the man beside her and felt calm sweep over her. She could sense that his dark thoughts about his past had impacted his life and who he had become as an adult. He was so kind and caring to everyone in his community that she was sure it was an overcompensation for what his family had been through, how his father had behaved, and of course what had happened to his mother. Another shooting star shot across the sky making an arc of bright light against the darkness.

'Let's make a wish, Goldie,' she said, loving the feel of his hand in hers.

'I hope that one day I make a better father than my dad,' he said quietly into the night sky.

'Goldie, you will make the most amazing father,' she squeezed his hand ever so slightly and tried to stop the tears from rolling down her face.

20

Chapter Twenty

As the fire died down, the only light was from the thin rays of the moon and the glow of the solar lamps in the camp kitchen. They stood beside her swag not wanting to end their night. Lara reached up her hand and cupped his cheek gently. 'I hope you understand that I need to take this slowly Curtis. I'm still getting over my last relationship.' He reached out and wrapped his arms around her small waist. 'I'm not him Lara. I would never hurt you. And if time is what you want then time is what I'll give you, because you are worth waiting for.' He pulled her closer and she nestled her head in that sweet spot just below his chin. *Oh why couldn't she just throw her towel into the ring and love this man with gay abandonment?* Reluctantly they went their separate ways. Lara unzipping her swag and crawling in. As she lay in bed on the thin mattress, her mind lingering on the wonderful kiss she had just had with Curtis. *Things are going to get very interesting,* she thought as she rolled over tucking her arm under her head. She could hear Curtis moving in his swag next door to her. She wondered what he was thinking. She was just so grateful that he had confided in her and that she could give him some comfort. Even though she had been through domestic violence herself it was hard to understand the toll it must have taken on a young Curtis and Janie. Now as adults they had to live with those horrific memories for the rest of their lives. A murdered father and a mother in jail. From the thin canvas of her bed she could hear Curtis tossing and turning in his sleeping bag. She supposed the night had stirred up lots of buried memories for him and realised that if they were to move forward with the relationship, she would have to learn to deal with his traumas.

When they jumped off the school bus and headed down the dusty lane way towards their home, Curtis felt the familiar gnawing anxiety reach the pit of his stomach. Two nights ago, Janie and he had crawled into their hiding space and listened while their father berated their mother. At one point Janie had put her hands over Curtis's ears so that he wouldn't hear their mother scream.

'Look Curtie, it's a dandelion. Here, put your head back and I'll see if you like butter or not.' Janie approached him with the yellow weed in her hand. Curtis stopped walking and put his little head right back, exposing his soft white neck so that Janie could place the weed near it. 'Yep, you don't just like butter Curt, you love it,' she laughed.

'Here let me do it to you,' he said, jumping up and down with excitement.

Janie knelt down on the ground and gave the weed to her brother. Suddenly she wrapped her arms around him and whispered. 'I love you Curtie boy.' The two of them stayed like that for a while not wanting to go home and face whatever it was they were to face that night, be it a violent father or a bruised mother.

'Quick Curtis follow me,' said Janie in a whisper, trying not to draw attention to herself. She took his hand and ran down the hallway to the wardrobe in their shared bedroom. 'Bring Wawa with you.' Their mother had placed blankets, bottles of water, some dry biscuits and a night light inside the wardrobe as a safe hiding spot for the children to go to when their father was in a rage. Curtis hugged Wawa the koala to him and put his head on Janie's knee. 'It's okay little man, he won't find us in here. You are safe now.' Janie patted Curtis gently on the back trying to feel as confident as her words sounded. She pulled a blanket from the floor and draped it over the two of them for warmth. The glow of the rocket night light sent an eerie yellow tinge over the small space. In the distance and through the thin wooden door they could hear their father shouting and banging things around in the kitchen. The rage had come on so suddenly that, this time, it took their mother by surprise. One minute she was cooking the family meal of chops and mash and the next it was thrown up against the kitchen wall. Their father towered menacingly over their cowering mother. She yelled at Janie to go and hide just as their father slapped her hard against her cheek. Janie took Curtis's hand and they ran, but not before they heard the terrible thud his strike made. There was no rhyme nor reason to his rages now; they were becoming more frequent and more violent. Janie listened to Curtis's breath becoming more regulated and opened up a bottle of water for him to drink. Suddenly through the thin wood they heard their bedroom door slam open with a splintering sound. Janie quickly turned off the night light leaving them in an inky blackness. Curtis sat up with eyes wide and terrified. They could hear their father angrily shouting for them followed by their mother's voice as she tried to lure him out of their bedroom. Janie and Curtis held their breath and sank back into the depth of the closet, trying to mould in with the hanging coats and pants. A trickle of warm urine soaked Curtis's pyjama pants as he wet himself in terror. Suddenly the closet door flung wide open and their father's fist grasped Janie's hair and yanked her from the closet. Curtis tried to hang on but their father was too strong. The closet door banged shut and Curtis heard the sound of the lock turn. Muffled screams and shouts came through the thin wood until all was quiet except for the small hiccupping of his cries. He lay in the dark in his wet pyjamas, too scared to put the night light back on in case he came back for him. He feared for Janie and his mother, not knowing what was happening to them outside of his locked door. *I should have held on tighter. I shouldn't have let her go. It's all my fault.* Cramp pained his legs and he tried to stretch out amongst the blankets. *Where was Janie,* he sobbed, wanting to be in her arms again. When sleep finally found him it was full of nightmares and boogie monsters.

He was awakened in the morning by Janie carefully unlocking the door and helping him out. She looked a fright; her hair was a mess and her eyes were red rimmed and wide with fear. 'Come on Curtis we have to get ready for school.'

'What happened Janie, are you okay?' Curtis sobbed and grabbed Janie's arm to help him out of the closet, he noticed her wince at the sudden pain it had caused her.

'Never mind that now, we have to go. Mum wants us out of the house.' She hurriedly dressed him and then pulled on her own pants and top. Their mother had her back to them when they walked into the kitchen to say goodbye. He remembered walking up to her and wrapping his little arms around her legs, burying his head into her back. She turned quickly kneeling down so that they were face to face. She gave him a tight hug. He remembered the ugly brownish, bruising around her eye and cheek. His poor mother deserved so much better; they all did. 'Take care my lovely boy and girl. Remember I will always love you.' The three embraced not realising that that would be the last time they would all be together. Curtis and Janie walked the half mile to the bus stop to wait for the school bus. When they got to school, a kind teacher took them to the staffroom and made them hot toast with jam and sweet tea. She gently washed their faces and read them a picture story book until the bell went to start the day. Many of the staff knew what was going on in their home but they felt powerless to get involved. At recess, when Curtis ate an apple the kindly teacher had given him, he was taunted by the older boys for being dirty and poor. The Olsen brothers were the worst offenders, but when they went for Janie, Curtis charged at them kicking and biting. He was taken from the yard and given an in-house suspension. That was the day their aunty picked them up from school and they never saw their mum and dad again.

21

Chapter Twenty-one

Lara woke the next morning feeling relaxed and rested. Through the netting on her swag, she looked out at the expansive blue sky above her, remembering parts of what happened last night, from her first kiss with Curtis to his opening up to her about his parents. It broke her heart to know what he and Janie had been through as small children. She thought of her own childhood; safe, protected, and loved.

She could hear Curtis humming to himself as he got the fire started for a morning cup of tea. She rolled out of her swag and stretched her hands up into the sky. It was a beautiful spring day. She put on her Blundstones and made her way to the fire. 'Good morning Goldie, how did you sleep?' she said, sitting down on her camp chair.

'Not that great actually, I think our talk brought up some terrible nightmares. Anyway, how did you sleep?'

'I'm sorry to hear that Curtis, I thought I could hear you tossing during the night.' She gave him a sympathetic look. 'I have to say that I loved being in my swag, it's so comfortable. I would never have thought sleeping under the stars could be so good; when I was living in Melbourne, I was forever cooped up inside. Hey, do you need a hand with anything?' She noticed he had put on a pan of fried eggs and was buttering rolls.

'Nah I'm all good Lars, we have egg and bacon rolls for brekky and then if you're okay with that we can head off to the Anderson's farm. Then we can hit, Henderson's Lookout.'

Two hours later they were pulling into a remote farmhouse on the border of Victoria and South Australia. The vibrations of the cattle grate woke her out of her daydreaming and she sat up higher to have a look around at the beautiful landscape.

'Wow, I forgot that people actually live like this. I would miss the shops and just popping out for milk and bread.' She looked around and saw the lush green grass and willow trees that were fed by the Murray River.

'Yeah, I know but some people love the country isolation.'

They made their way up the long gravel driveway, turned a sharp bend, and ended up at a white picket fenced homestead of grey and white. The verandas swept around the house hugging it like a dear friend. The front door was painted a welcoming light blue colour and on either side of the path were standard roses that Lara could see were well-tended and looked after. The house seemed to go on forever, with what looked like added rooms here and there. The iron roof reflected the light of the spring sun and a flock of cockatoos landed in a willow tree in the front yard, singing their hello calls for all to hear. A red cattle dog came out to welcome them and ran circles around the car, his big red tongue sticking out the side of his mouth.

'Oh here comes Dave Anderson, hop out and I'll introduce you.' Curtis jumped out of the ute and went to shake Dave's hand. 'Hey Dave, nice to see you again. This is Lara Benton, a friend of mine,' he said, introducing Lara to Dave Anderson.

The red cattle dog stopped to sniff Lara's boots and she bent down to give him a scratch behind the ear. 'Hi Dave, nice to meet you,' she said warmly.

Dave smiled at Lara and shook her small hand in his big calloused one. 'Alice has just put the billy on, come in and have a cuppa. I'll show you the damaged shed later. Settle down Big Red,' he said to the kelpie, and turned towards the house. Curtis and Lara followed, with Big Red close at their heels.

The house smelt of cookie dough and lavender and Lara's salivary glands started to work on overdrive. 'Something smells delicious,' she said, following Dave into the country kitchen and smiling happily as Dave introduced her to Alice.

'Come in, we don't get many visitors out here. Take a seat. How do you like your tea?' said a very over excited Alice, smiling warmly back at Lara. Lara could see that she was heavily pregnant and wondered who on earth was going to deliver the baby when the time came.

They stayed for an hour talking about all things farming and some of the town gossip. Alice was curious to know about the shopping spree Lara had taken with Tiffany to Adelaide a few weekends ago. Lara didn't think she could cope with the isolation that Alice endured, and it made her think of Curtis when he was young and how his family had lived hours away from the nearest town. Isolation was certainly a big part of a farmer's life if they didn't live near a town.

When the men left to take photos of the burnt shed Lara and Alice walked out onto the beautiful veranda. 'So Alice when are you due; do you have a plan for when the baby comes; how far away is the nearest hospital?' Lara took a seat in one of the old cane chairs.

'I'm leaving on Monday to stay at my sister's place in Pinnaroo. They have a small hospital there that deliver babies as well as everything else hospitals do.'

'Perfect Alice that's so good having a hospital there for you and your baby and it's not that far away.'

When they finally made it to Henderson's Lookout it was everything and more that Curtis had talked about. The red outcrop of rock looked almost prehistoric in its shape and colour. One side of the cliff dropped off falling into a beautiful tree filled valley below. The light blue water was so clear that Lara could see little fish darting in and out of the rocks and plants. The water was freezing but refreshing in the noon sun. She swam over to the small waterfall that cascaded down the orange rocks and sat on a ledge of stone, sunning herself like a goanna to get warm. Lara looked up at the blue sky and powder puff clouds and felt a peace settle upon her. She watched Curtis swimming, his powerful arms pulling him closer towards her, hardly making a ripple in the water. Suddenly he was balancing next to her on the rocky outcrop, so close that his skin touched her skin as they both tried to warm their bodies. Later they picnicked on cheese and biscuits and enjoyed the chocolate chip cookies that Alice had generously provided them. They drank the last of their beer, the cold fizz going down a treat cooling their hot bodies.

'Thanks so much for bringing me here, Goldie, it's so lovely to see different parts of the country.' She laid back on the smooth boulder, putting her arm across her eyes to block out the sun. She was dressed in her black one-piece bathers with her hair up in a high ponytail. She had on a pink cap which set off her olive skin, her ponytail popping through the hole in the back. Curtis looked down at her and she felt his eyes wandering across her body, stopping at her face and smiling widely.

'I knew you would love it, Lars. But I reckon if we are to get back to River Bend before midnight we should leave now.'

22

Chapter Twenty-two

The excursion to the Talbot Historical Museum and picnic was taking place on Monday so Lara had stayed back at school to go through the paperwork. The museum might be a bit dry for the students but she reasoned that afterwards there was a huge playground in Talbot she planned to take them to for lunch and an hour-long play on the equipment. It was her first excursion and she was both excited and nervous to be taking the twenty-two children and two parent volunteers on a bus to see how towns in the local area were in the 1900s. They were doing a topic called 'Now and Then', and the children were very enthusiastic about it. She noticed that she was one excursion notice down. *Oh no,* she thought, little Tom hadn't brought his back. Even though it was after hours on Friday night, she went to the office and found his phone number but when the call was answered there was just a muffling sound at the end of the line. *Poor little Tom won't be able to go unless I get this signed.* She wrote down his address and jumped in her car to drive east to Bard Road.

The countryside turned from the green of the river to the red dirt of country Victoria. This was sheep country, and the persistent drought had hit the farmers hard. Lara thought about Tom as she drove along the deserted road. He was a quiet boy with large brown eyes and a cheeky smile, when he dared to share it. Lara felt he was gaining in confidence as the weeks went by. He was clean, but dressed like his clothes had been rolling around in the backyard for a time, a little bit stained and creased. His lunch box was minimal, nothing she felt she should report, but definitely no love like Elsie's that had handwritten notes from Tiffany on her banana like, 'Mummy loves you', which made Lara smile. No, Tom was just a little bit ragged and tired looking, but nothing she could have reported. She hadn't been east before, and it was amazing how the landscape changed in a dramatic way. When she got to the old homestead she noticed that it was quite run down, with the front yard bursting with yellow daisies and thistles. A lone black cockatoo sat on a peeling white ghost gum smashing gum nuts in its powerful beak. A family of noisy miners made a terrible racket on the electrical wires at the front of the property; almost like they were taunting her for being at this isolated country property alone. There was a deep veranda at the front of the house which looked like it wrapped around the whole structure but sagged in places. The two front windows on either side of the door had their shutters closed as if to say that strangers weren't welcome here, go away. There was an eeriness to the property that Lara hadn't seen or felt in River Bend before. With growing trepidation, she made her way around the weeds to the front door and timidly knocked. She waited, thinking she could hear a noise behind the door but no one answered. With the screech of the black cockatoos behind her Lara turned left and made her way around the sagging veranda. She maneuvered her way around an old broken cane chair and looked through a small dirty window that framed a kitchen. Suddenly, her whole view was filled with a face that had eyes spread far apart and a nose that was flat beneath its broad forehead. Lara screamed and jumped back, nearly toppling over a dead pot plant. She held her chest and tried to massage her heart back into normal rhythm. She heard a noise behind her and turned quickly to find little Tom Wilson standing there.

'Miss Benton, what are you doing here?' He asked, his eyes darted from her to the window.

'Tom, I'm sorry I got a fright. Who is that in the window?' she pointed a shaky hand to the glass pane.

From behind Tom a young boy who appeared to have Down Syndrome appeared. 'Ello,' he said, in a wide toothy grin 'I'm Bill. I'm Bill and that's Tom,' he said, pointing to Tom.

Lara regained her composure and put a hand through her hair trying to pull herself back into the role of sensible teacher. 'Hello Bill, I'm Miss Benton, Tom's teacher, and it's lovely to meet you even if you did give me a big fright through the window just now.'

'Haaa, Bill scared Miss,' he said, in a husky voice, clapping his hands together in glee.

'Miss. Benton, am I in trouble?' Tom said and hung his head sadly.

'No of course not Tom, where's your father? I need him to sign your excursion note so that you can come on the trip with us.'

'He's at work, Miss. Benton.'

'When will he be home? I can wait and then get him to sign the form.'

Just then the sound of a truck could be heard coming up the old gravel road from behind the house.

'It's Dad, it's Dad,' yelled Bill, running towards the sound.

Tom and Lara followed him around the side of the house where a large semi-trailer pulled up. Bill was jumping up and down with excitement when a blonde-haired man in dark blue overalls jumped out and gave Bill a big bear hug.

'How are my boys?' he said warmly, as he turned around to stare at Lara. 'Who's this then?' He asked in confusion, his brow scrunched up into one.

'Hello Mr. Wilson, I'm Tom's teacher, Lara Benton,' she cleared her throat and extended her hand.

'Oh, okay I'm the boy's father Sam Wilson. Nice to meet you,' he clasped her hand and gave it a shy shake. 'What can I do for you?' he asked, suspiciously looking from Tom to Lara and back to Bill.

'Oh, it's nothing,' she stammered. 'I just hoped you'd sign this form so that Tom can come on our excursion Monday.' She held out the note for him to see.

He grabbed a pen from his shirt pocket and quickly signed the form, handing it back to her.

'Well, thank you Mr. Wilson, um I will see Tom at school. Bye Bill, bye Tom,' she said, with a wave of her hand.

'Bye Miss. Benton,' both the boys said in unison.

As she headed towards her car, she could feel Sam Wilson's eyes practically digging into her back. *That was strange,* she thought, *not a thank you to be heard and certainly not the country welcome I had been expecting.* She started her car and turned around to give another wave, but the little party of three had disappeared into the old cottage.

23

Chapter Twenty-three

On Sunday afternoon Janie was just putting the closed sign on the window of the cafe as Lara was walking back from the IGA, swinging her cotton bag of shopping. 'Hi stranger, how's things? Come on in and let's do Sunday Sippers,' she said, in her sing-song voice.

'Sunday Sippers, I love it.' Lara followed Janie into the cafe and took up a spot on one of the comfy couches out in the courtyard. Janie produced a bottle of Riesling and two glasses and plonked them down on the coffee table.

'So how are things, Lara?' she asked, pouring two glasses of wine.

'Really good, thanks Janie. I'm a bit nervous as I have my first excursion tomorrow to the Talbot Museum. I'll bring the wine next Sunday, you always supply.'

Janie dismissed Lara's last comment with a wave of her hand and said, 'That sounds riveting, taking twenty-something kids on a bus to Talbot. Shoot me now,' laughing, she picked up her glass by the stem and twirled the pale yellow liquid.

'Yes, well all part of the package I'm afraid. But honestly Janie, they are such great kids I'm sure it will be fine. And we plan on spending the afternoon at that huge park in Talbot central.'

'That sounds a bit more like it. What else have you been up to?'

'Not that much really, just working.' Lara's mind quickly switched to Tom. 'Hey do you know anything about the Wilson's that live on

Bard Road?' she asked, and took a delicious sip. 'Oh, I think I like Sunday Sippers.'

'No, I don't think I've ever met them. They weren't at the Australia Day picnic and I don't think they come into town much. Oh look here's Curtis, he might know.'

It had been a few days since Lara had seen Curtis and her heart did a silly flip thing in her chest as he walked through the door, his large bulk took up most of the door frame. She couldn't help thinking about the whipped cream incident and the wonderful stolen kiss at the camp site and felt the heat rise from her neck to her cheeks. Her lips started tingling and it wasn't from the wine. She quickly smoothed her hair behind her ear and sat up a little bit straighter.

'Might know who sis? Hi Lara, how's school?' he plonked down on the couch opposite her.

'Curtis do you want to try a new wine I'm thinking of getting for the cafe? Apparently it's very popular in Melbourne at the moment or so Joe Flinders told me,' Janie said, getting up and going into the café to get another wine glass. Janie was hoping to expand her business into serving locally produced wines for the lunch time rush. There was a growing interest in the local wineries in the area that as yet hadn't developed a food trade, so Janie saw it as the perfect opportunity to expand her business.

'When would I ever say no to a good drop of local wine? What about you Lara are you drinking that wine to celebrate a great week or commiserate the beginning of another one,' laughed Curtis, with a cheeky wink in Lara's direction.

'Didn't you know Curtis? We are celebrating Sunday Sippers, it's a new thing. I've actually had quite a week and it's not to do with my grade either.' She looked into Curtis's green eyes as they crinkled into a smile. 'Well actually it's about a student in my class,' said Lara, trying hard not to stare at Curtis's strong legs protruding from his work shorts. *Why does this man make my whole body react in an electrical way, tingling certain parts of my anatomy?* When he was around, Lara's senses seemed to be heightened.

'Yes Curt, do you know anything about the Wilson's out on Bard Road?' said Janie. She brought over a tray with a bowl of assorted nuts and some wedges of soft cheese.

'I know they only arrived late last year, apparently his wife died of cancer a few years ago... Tragic. Supposedly he's here to try and make a better life for him and his son in the country. I've met him a few times, he seems a nice enough bloke. Why?'

Lara told them about the meeting she had on Friday night.

'That's strange, there was never a mention of another child, only Tom,' he screwed up his face in confusion. 'And who looks after the boy when he's at work and Tom's at school? How old is he?'

'I don't know, um let's see... I would guess he was around about eight or nine. Please God don't tell me that he stays at home alone.' She held her hand to her heart. 'That might explain the not-so-warm welcome I received. I am taking it that there are no other schools in River Bend he could be going to?' She took a small sip of her drink, 'this is so delicious Janie.'

'Well I don't want to make assumptions but if he did need a special school, the closest to here would be in Charlotte's Bridge. That just wouldn't be feasible for anyone living in River Bend; it would take like three hours each way.'

'I think I'd better organise a meeting with Des and work out what our next step will be. We can't have a young boy staying at that cottage on his own every day.' Lara shook her head.

'Well let me know if I can do anything Lara. I feel sorry for them, but the father cannot expect that it's acceptable to keep his young child at home alone,' he said, also shaking his head slowly.

Lara loved the compassion that Curtis showed for the people in his community.

'So Lara I ran into Josh this morning. What's the story there, he's like a bad smell that won't go away?' Janie spread some soft cheese on her biscuit and sat back down on the couch, tucking her legs up under her bottom.

'Jeez, I swear he was meant to be going back to Melbourne. What's he up to, I wonder? Believe me Janie, as I told you at the pub, there is definitely *no* us and he is *not* a very nice man, even though he appears to act perfectly,' she said, shaking her head at Janie.

'Good to know Lara,' Janie said, 'what an idiot hanging around like that when you have clearly told him to buzz off.' She picked up some nuts from the bowl and put them daintily into her mouth.

'I was there Janie, and Lara could not have been more direct and honest with him. Remember Lara, if he starts harassing you, I'd love to slap an AVO on him. It would ...make my day,' Curtis said with menace, trying to imitate Clint Eastward.

Lara could see a muscle twitch on his left cheek as he clenched his jaw in anger. 'Believe me Curtis, if he dares to come near me, I will definitely take you up on your offer. I just can't understand why he hasn't left town. I will not be threatened by him again,' she said, with a determined look in her eye.

Just then Curtis's phone started to buzz. He looked at the screen and screwed his eyes up in confusion. 'Sorry ladies I have to take this.' He got up and walked into the café.

Janie reached over and patted Lara's knee, 'I'm so sorry you had to go through all that with Josh Lara. Covid must have been an even bigger nightmare for you.'

'You have no idea Janie but honestly, I'll never let him, or any man, treat me like that again. I can't believe I stayed with him for two years. I look back on that time and just want to shake myself into reality,' she said, pulling her mouth into a straight line.

'You have definitely escaped him and if the creep doesn't leave soon, I'll sic the bloody town onto him.' Janie filled Lara's glass.

'He wouldn't want to get on the wrong side of Pearl or Shirl,' said Curtis, coming back in to join the conversation. He sat down next to Lara on the couch, his thigh brushing against hers.

It sent a shiver down her backbone and a warm feeling to the pit of her stomach.

'Who was that?' asked Janie.

'Oh, there is no privacy in this café,' laughed Curtis. Then in a more serious voice. 'If you want to know Miss Nosey, there's been a development in the snowdropper case. Barrington has just arrested a man and I don't think you are going to be happy when you find out who it is...'

24

Chapter Twenty-four

'What do you mean Curtis? Who is it?' Lara was confused.

'I am only telling you this because Barrington wants you to come down to the station. He has arrested Sam Wilson on suspicion of theft and has him in custody, which means the boys have no one to look after them.'

Lara opened and closed her mouth like a stunned mullet. 'What!' she stammered. 'You have to be absolutely joking, Sam Wilson?' She shook her head in disbelief. 'I think I'm in shock Curtis! I only met the man once, but the snowdropper? I just didn't get that vibe.'

Curtis put his hand out to help her up off the couch and the two of them walked towards the front door. Even though Lara knew there was a disaster waiting in the wings for little Tom and his family, she couldn't help the warm feeling that flowed through her veins at the thought of working with Curtis. She also couldn't help remembering the feel of his soft lips on hers and how she had wanted it to go further.

'Listen guys, ring me when you find out what's going on. I'll leave you something to eat in the cafe kitchen if you're not home by dinner time,' said Janie.

Lara and Curtis walked to the police station, quietly discussing what they should do with the boys if Sam was held overnight.

Curtis said, 'I think I might give Marg a ring, she'll know what to do. She was a social worker before she retired. She is also our volunteer 'out of home care' contact. We have only had to call upon her once before when a farmer out on the west side had too many beers and beat his wife, the coward. Marg took in the three children. She's amazing.' Curtis pulled his phone from of his pocket.

'I didn't know that Marg volunteered? She told me about Dave and her social work career. He seemed like such a lovely man,' replied Lara.

'Yeah, I think the whole town went to the funeral. It was just so unexpected; he was such a big strong man. Marg's still grieving and trying to find her feet without him. She sold the farm after he died and now lives alone in a beautiful cottage by the river. Have you been there?' Lara nodded and Curtis went on, 'She also volunteers at the community centre running a playgroup twice a week, as well as counselling some of the women in the area, and then of course everything else she does for this town.'

As they got to the police station Curtis talked with Marg on the phone. Lara couldn't distinguish anything Marg was saying. When he hung up, he ushered Lara through the front door.

'Miss Benton, what are you doing here?' asked Tom, with a sob. His eyes were bloodshot as if he had been crying.

'Hi Miss, it's me Bill,' said the young boy. He approached Lara with a big toothy grin and grabbed her hand. *God,* thought Lara, *he's got no idea what trouble his little family is in.*

'Alright Lara, can you stay here with the boys? I will go and sort out the paperwork and check in on Sam and Sarge and see what is exactly going on here,' said Curtis, in a professional voice. 'Marg should be here soon. She's gone to the farm to get some clothes and supplies and said she will be here ASAP.'

'Okay Curtis but do you think I could take the boys back to my place so that they can have something to eat and sit on a comfortable couch instead of these hard plastic chairs?' Lara asked concerned.

'Perfect Lara, that sounds like a plan. I will text Marg to tell her to go straight to your place.'

Once back in her apartment Lara started to heat up an early dinner of baked beans and a couple of fried eggs. She put the toast in the toaster and turned around to look at the boys as they were sitting at her table doing a drawing. Bill was totally engrossed in his picture but poor little Tom was looking around the place like he was a deer caught in the headlights. Lara took the food over to them and with a gentle smile placed it on the mats in front of them. They clearly hadn't eaten for a while; they wolfed down the simple meal with relish.

'Okay, I think some ice-cream and topping is in order here since you boys ate all your dinner.' She scooped out large spheres of vanilla ice-cream and topped it with Marg's homemade strawberry jam. Tom thanked her but just stared into the bowl. He was quite subdued, probably realising that his dad was in a lot of trouble. Young Bill looked at his dessert as though it were an adventure, picked up the silver spoon and started shovelling the gooey substance into his mouth. When there was a knock on the door Tom looked up quickly with bright eyes, but when Lara answered it Marg was standing there carrying a colourful carpet bag, Tom's face crumbled into sadness. It just about broke Lara's heart to see him so unhappy.

'Hi Lara, hi boys. My name is Marg, and I've brought some of your things from home so that you don't feel so scared and alone. Now I found this on someone's bed. Is it Mr. Bunny?' she said, in a quiet, gentle voice.

'That's my Bunny Man,' said a happy little Bill, he came over and grabbed the bunny from Marg's hand and gave him a loving hug.

'So, who is this then?' She pulled out a Shrek doll from her enormous, Mary Poppins type bag.

'That's Tom's favourite dolly,' yelled Bill. He pointed excitedly to the small doll Marg held in her hand.

'That's not mine! I don't know where it came from,' said a mortified Tom, tears formed at the corner of his eyes.

Oh the poor little thing. He's embarrassed to have a doll on his bed, thought Lara, stepping over to Tom and putting an arm around him. 'It's fine Tom, don't stress. Around here somewhere I still have my blanky that I had when I was a child. It can be our little secret, as long as you don't tell anyone that I have a blanky, of course,' she smiled at the young boy and witnessed him practically letting out a huge breath of air in relief. How astute of Marg to bring these special things from the boys' home. Lara would never have thought to do such a simple but comforting thing.

'Well first things first,' said Marg. 'I've got a lovely room set up in my house just down the road with a double bed in it, that is if you boys don't mind sharing,' said Marg.

'Yeah, yeah we can share,' said an ecstatic Bill.

'What time do the boys have to be at the excursion Lara?'

'The bus is leaving at 9.30, but Bill doesn't go to our school. Would you be able to take care of him just until we find out what's happening with his dad,' said Lara, packing away the dirty dishes as the boys collected their shoes to put on.

'No problem, Bill and I can go to playgroup tomorrow,' she turned to face Bill. 'You can be my big helper with the little children tomorrow as I always go to playgroup on Mondays.'

'Bill can be a big helper,' he said, gleefully.

'Come on then boys my car is parked out the front,' said Marg.

'Do you mind if I follow you Marg. I just feel that Tom might need a familiar face around when he goes to bed,' whispered Lara, as the boys went to the rust-coloured couch to put on their shoes.

'Brilliant idea Lara,' said Marg, patting Lara gently on the arm. 'It will be good for them to have you there.'

Lara was in the bedroom reading a story to the boys when Curtis crept in.

'Hi guys, do you mind if I listen to the story? It's been a long time since anyone read me one and it seems like fun,' he said, squishing Bill over and lying down next to him on the bed. Lara thought what a wonderful father Curtis would make and couldn't help feeling sad as she thought about what his father had done and what he had witnessed as a young boy. It amazed her that he was so together after what he had been through.

'It's Policeman Gold, yeah you can listen with us,' said a tired Bill, stifling a large yawn.

Young Tom looked over and asked in a quiet voice, 'How's Dad?'

'All good mate, he's settled for the night. Had some dinner and is now lying in his bed but he did ask me to give you both a big high five,' said Curtis, lifting up his hand for the two boys to slap.

Lara looked at Curtis, so glad that he was there to reassure the boys that their dad was okay. Well at least for tonight, but the boys didn't need to know about what may or may not happen tomorrow. She couldn't help but think how different Curtis was from Josh. They were actually worlds apart. Josh would never have taken the time to come and make sure the boys were settled let alone give them a reassuring word from their dad. 'Okay,' said Lara, 'everyone settle down, get comfy, pull up the covers and I will continue with this lovely story.'

25

Chapter Twenty-five

After Lara had got the boys settled into Marg's spare room she jumped in her car and headed back home. Curtis had left to check in on Sam and let him know his boys were being taken care of. She heard her stomach growl and realised she hadn't eaten since lunchtime. When she got home, she put away her bag and headed down the back stairs to the dark cafe using her house keys to open up. Turning on the light over the oven she got out a salad and quiche from the industrial fridge and set about making a plate for herself. Suddenly there was a tapping on the window and Curtis stood at the door waiting to be let in. 'Hi Curtis come in; what's going on with Sam?' Lara made up another plate and stuck the quiche in the microwave.

'Sergeant Barrington, apparently, got an anonymous tip off that Sam had been seen near the last theft of underwear and did a raid on his house and found some ladies' lingerie in a shed out the back.'

'What's Sam saying?' She brought the plates over to the small table by the door.

'Of course, he's denying it. He's in the lockup overnight and he has used his one phone call to call a lawyer in the city who will get here tomorrow afternoon.' Curtis tucked into his salad and quiche. 'God I'm starving,' he said through a mouth full of green leaves.

'I just don't know Curtis. I only met the guy for all of five minutes, but he just doesn't seem like the type to take ladies' underwear,' she said, shaking her head slowly.

'How did the boys go?' he asked, ignoring her statement.

'Great, Marg was unreal. She handled the whole situation like a pro. She is going to drop Tom off at school tomorrow for the excursion and take Bill with her for the day. She's bloody amazing and a Godsend,' said Lara, collecting the dirty dishes and putting them in the dishwasher.

Curtis got up out of his seat and went to the fridge searching for another beer.

'Here Lara, do you want me to top up your wine?' He held the bottle aloft and looked over to where she was at the sink.

'Nah thanks Curtis, I have a big day tomorrow. I think I will catch an early night.' As she maneuvered past him to get to the back door, he turned from the fridge and bumped right into her, his sharp elbow hitting her left boob.

'Ouch,' she said, putting her hand up to massage her breast.

'I'm so sorry Lara. God, are you alright?' He grabbed her by the shoulder and turned her towards him. Tears sprang up in the corner of her eyes. 'Jeez, Lars I'm so sorry,' he pulled her into a bear hug, rubbing his knuckles gently up and down her back making soothing noises.

'Oh, Curtis it's honestly not that, I'm just feeling so sad for Tom and Bill. This should not be happening to them, they are so little and scared,' she sobbed into his strong shoulder. The feel of his arms around her left her weak at the knees. She reached around his taut body and placed her palms flat against the hard muscle of his back, the feel of the cotton material under her hands a comfort. With her breasts pushed against his chest, her nipples became hard and sensitive to the feel of his body so close to her.

He slowly reached under her chin and tipped her head up so that she was looking directly into his brilliant green eyes. She was so close she could see the tiny crease lines around his mouth as he looked into the depths of her eyes. He reached up slowly with his finger and gently wiped the tears away, all the time staring at her with a longing look. The feel of his fingertips upon her soft skin sent a rolling shudder down her body, ending somewhere just below her belly. He moved his finger to gently touch the outline of her mouth, moving sensually over the soft pink of her skin. She could taste the salty tears as her tongue came out to lick the tip of his finger. Slowly his hand moved down to caress her chin and neck, her head arched back so that his hand was free to travel at will, their eyes locked all the while.

She was drowning, staring into the very heart of him. *Oh my God,* thought Lara as his hand came around and cupped the back of her head, gently pulling her lips towards his. She closed her eyes and a small moan escaped her parted mouth. *Oh my I want this man,* she thought as their lips met. Somewhere in the back of her mind that little voice said, *Lara, what are you doing?* But it was pushed away by the pure lust that raged through her body and made every nerve from her fingers to her toes scream with sensitivity. She reached up and cupped the back of his head, parting her lips so that his tongue could explore every inch of her mouth. She welcomed him in with a deep intensity, as her mouth moved to the rhythm of his mouth. She was losing herself in him.

Slowly, he pulled back from her and looked directly into her eyes. 'God Lara, are you sure?' he said, in a breathless sexy voice. 'I don't think I can stop again with just a kiss; I want you so much.' Lara felt herself nod as she took one of his hands, placed it slowly to her lips and kissed every fingertip in turn, all the while never taking her eyes from his. He once again embraced her, his hands slowly moving over every bump in her spine. She stood back and pulled her t-shirt over her head, exposing a lacy white bra that glowed in the soft lighting. His fingers played with the lace before working their way under the material until his warm hand found her erect nipple. He pulled the flimsy material away and bent his head.

She melted into him, small moans escaping her parted lips. 'I want you.' She pulled at his shirt, wanting to feel the nakedness of him, wanting his skin on hers. He quickly retrieved his wallet from his pocket, pulled out a condom and put it on the bench in front of them. He pulled his t-shirt over his head in a swift motion and with one hand undid his shorts and let them fall to the floor. His hardness escaped and she let out a small whimper. After applying the condom, he pushed her up against the bench and pulled her shorts and undies off in one swoop.

Slowly he entered her. He moaned in her ear, his hot breath tickling her lobe. 'Lara,' he moaned. Faster he moved inside her until an electric shock coursed through her body and she screamed out his name, tremor after tremor moved from her toes to her core. 'Curtis,' she sobbed against his sweat fuelled body. The orgasm continued rumbling in that special place. Suddenly he pushed his head back and cried out her name. She felt a great shudder and she moaned loudly in the silent room. He picked her up and cradled her. 'Curtis,' she moaned into his ear, kissing his cheek. 'I can't get enough of you. I want you all.'

Gently he walked her over to the couch where he put her down and lay next to her. He got up on his elbows and looked into her eyes. She reached up and cupped his face, kissing him deeply with a lust that threatened to explode from her lower body, she felt a tickling warmth fill her again. When the next orgasm came, they clung together, calling out each other's names in guttural, primal voices, sweat pooling around their bodies. When they were finally sated, they lay with their bodies pushed against each other; skin on naked skin, a perfect fit. Fire on fire. She wanted to stay like this forever. He slowly nuzzled into her neck kissing her soft sensitive skin. He was hers and she was his, they were one.

After a while they got up and dressed, holding hands like teenagers as they made their way up to her apartment. Neither were ready to end this incredible night and all Lara wanted was to feel him lying naked next to her in her bed. They lay side by side, talking into the night. He told her how he'd had feelings for her that very first day he saw her in the main street of River Bend. She told him how she had been attracted to him, but the horrible memories of Josh had gotten in the way. He fell asleep spooning her and she lay in his arms listening to his even breathing, her eyes closed, with a contented smile on her face.

She woke up the next morning in a haze of euphoria. She reached across but the spot where he had slept was cold. On the pillow there was a note that read.

Had to go in to work early and didn't want to wake you. Can't wait to see you tonight! I hope the excursion is a success.

Love, C xxxx

She rolled over and clutched the letter to her breast, smiling secretly to herself as she remembered the antics from last night. Just then her alarm went off but Lara gave herself the luxury of one more read of the note, paying particular attention to the word love, before she jumped into the shower. While she shampooed her hair she thought again about their night. She had only ever been with two other men. When she was in Greece, she'd had a drunken ride on the back of a local's motorbike and ended up in her tent with him. It had been rushed and messy. Not perfect, but it let out a lot of pent-up emotions for her. Then of course there was Josh. Selfish to the last gasp, sex had been all about his pleasure. Last night, things were so different. Curtis had aroused her in a way that she had never known possible. She blushed slightly as she remembered the things his tongue could do. *Oh my God Lara, get a grip. You are about to take twenty-two kids on your first ever excursion and you are thinking about sex.* She laughed and combed conditioner through her long hair with her fingers.

26

Chapter Twenty-six

Of course, the excursion was a huge success and everyone, including little Tom, had a great time. The playground was exactly what the children needed after being in the museum for an hour. They were surprisingly attentive to learning about their area in the early days, but nothing quite beat the big slide and flying fox. When it was time to head back to school the old bus driver, Mr. Barry, hauled himself into the seat and started up the engine. 'Did you kids have a great day?' he said, over the loudspeaker, and all the children cheered. Lara felt so relieved that they had all enjoyed it. *Tick, first excursion a success,* she thought.

When they got back to school Marg was waiting for them with a very excited Bill. 'Lara, I've made an appointment with Des to talk about getting Bill enrolled into the school. I may be able to access some funding for an aide to help him out in the classroom. I haven't spoken to Bill's dad yet, but this can be an emergency placement,' said Marg, watching Tom and Bill having fun in the playground. The other children got back on Mr. Barry's bus to be taken to their various stops in town.

'Bill and Tom can stay with me until the meetings over Marg.' Lara, waved for the boys to join her in her classroom.

'Tom, what would you like to do? I have some colouring sheets, or you can go on the iPad if you like.'

'Colour, colour in please,' interrupted Bill. Lara set up one of the tables with some crayons and pencils for the boys to use while she filed the paperwork from the excursion.

When her meeting was over Marg came to Lara's room where Tom and Bill were concentrating on finishing some mindful colouring-in sheets. 'How did it go Marg?' asked Lara, as she started to pack up her computer to take home.

'I really think it's going to work out okay for the family if, of course, Dad doesn't get arrested and put in you know where,' whispered Marg, trying not to let Tom overhear the conversation. 'I spoke to Curtis and he thinks, even if Sam does get a guilty verdict, there won't be any jail time as it's a first offence. Anyway, Des has put in for emergency funding and young Bill can start in your room tomorrow. I said I would volunteer to help until he can get you a Learning Support Officer to help you.'

'Marg that is incredible. I just wish Sam had known that this was an option when he came to River Bend. Then he wouldn't have had poor Bill stay at the property on his own all that time.' Lara shook her head in wonderment at the realisation that poor Sam must not have had any support from anyone when his wife passed away.

Lara went back to Marg's cottage to help get the boys settled before jumping in her car and heading back home. She was relaxing on her balcony with a cuppa waiting for Curtis to call in after work. She was enjoying the last rays of the sun when a movement down on the street distracted her. Standing over the road was the hoodie guy. It had been months since her last sighting of him and she felt the hairs on her arms rise. He was looking up at her balcony, staring at her. *Bloody hell, what is this guy's problem?* she thought as she stood to get a better look at his features so that she could tell Curtis. When he saw her stand, he took off past the IGA and down the alleyway again. She took the stairs two at a time and quickly followed him. The alley was deserted this time of day, but she made her way along it until she came to the carpark out the back. There were a few cars there but no sign of the man. *Interesting,* she thought as she realised that the back door of the Olsen Brothers Hardware and Feed Store opened onto the park. She gingerly crept over to the door and held her breath, listening to see if she could hear anything.

It was all silent. She continued walking past the feed store and noticed some shipping containers dotted around the back of the car park. There was also a huge tin shed out the back and one of its old green roller doors was up. From where she was standing, Lara could just make out the front wheel of what looked like a truck. She walked closer and with a start realised that it was the same semi she had seen the first time she saw the man in the hoodie. The logo on the side read Olsen Brothers and it looked to be about the same size as the truck that she had seen. She walked closer into the shed and saw what looked like hundreds of boxes piled up on wooden pellets on the concrete floor. *What could they possibly be transporting in all of these boxes,* she thought? *Surely not pet food or nuts and bolts, there are way too many boxes,* she furrowed her brow in thought. As she moved around the back of the truck, she heard voices coming from outside the shed. *Bloody hell,* she thought, and ducked behind one of the tallest stacks of boxes, crouching down on her knees.

'Listen here Bart, if that driver of yours does anything stupid I'll bloody kill him myself. I have fixed it this time but there is not going to be a next time. And the bloody guy I used as a scapegoat had a freaking disabled kid at home that no one knew about and now the Department of Health and Human Services is sniffing around. It's a bloody disaster. Do you hear me, a bloody disaster?' Lara's blood turned to ice. *Damn that was the same voice she had heard in the feed store, surely it wasn't...*Very slowly, Lara peaked around the edge of the box to try and see if the man talking to Bart was who she thought it was. *Jeez no,* thought Lara, *it is bloody Sergeant Barrington!* Lara quickly ducked back behind the boxes, pushing her body against them in the hopes she would disappear. She had a sick feeling in her stomach and had to consciously try to keep her breathing regulated. *He's set the whole thing up and Sam is the fall guy, but why?* She held her breath, realising that if she were caught eavesdropping, she would be in a whole world of trouble. *Whatever these two guys are up to it is definitely not good!*

'Now go and get Zammit and tell him to start packing all these boxes into the truck. I want this stuff out of my town ASAP,' said Barrington.

She heard the roller door shutter close and shivered in the gloom. She clasped her hands together trying to stop them from shaking. She had to get out of this shed.

In the dappled light she quietly made her way around the side of the truck walking towards the doors. She reached down to pull up the roller door. She pulled, but it would not budge, they had locked it. *Damn,* she chewed at her bottom lip. Reaching around to her back pocket she realised she had left her mobile on the table next to her cup of tea. *Okay, think Lara...* Suddenly, light filled the shed and the roller door was hefted up. She pushed her body against the side of the truck and prayed that whoever had arrived went to the left and not the right. She heard their footsteps walk up the opposite side of the truck. Using this opportunity to escape she snuck out the front roller door right smack bang into Bart Olsen.

'What the hell do we have here then,' said Bart, grabbing her forcefully by the arm and turning her around to face him. His face was so close to hers that she could see the brown cigarette stains on his teeth and smell the stale, day-old beer odour on his breath.

'Let me guess, you lost your cat?' he said, in a menacing voice.
God think Lara.

'I'm sorry Bart, I was actually going for a walk and I heard a noise coming from the shed, when I went in someone locked the roller door,' she stammered, hoping upon hope that Bart would believe her and not realise that she had overheard an important and very incriminating conversation.

'Sure, that's what happened. You're coming with me and don't you try and give me any trouble.' He pulled out a black gun from the waist of his jeans and pushed it in her ribs, 'you will be fish food for the feed store.' Lara froze with fear. She had never even seen a real gun let alone have one shoved in her side. He gave a laugh that turned into a growl and pushed her along towards the back of the hardware door. She looked from left to right, hoping that one of the Early twins or Patsy would come out of their buildings to save her. She saw where Patsy had the black towels hanging on a wire drying rack and willed her to come to the door to check if they were dry. But nobody came. When he got her inside, the gun still pointed in her face, he roughly pushed her onto a plastic dining chair. Bart put down the gun and grabbed some cable ties out of a drawer, then proceeded to bind Lara's hands and feet.

'Honestly Bart, I don't know what you are doing. I don't know anything. Please, just let me go,' she pleaded, hoping to find a softer side to him. At that moment Cam came from around the front of the store. 'What the hell, Bart,' he said, staring from Lara to Bart.

'I caught this one sneaking around the semi and eavesdropping on a very private conversation with Sergeant Barrington no less.'

'Christ man, what are you doing? Don't say his name out loud! Bloody hell, this is a disaster,' Cam said, raking his hands through his hair leaving the ends standing up. The whites of his eyes popped in shock at seeing Lara tied up.

'You stay here and I'll contact the Wolf Pack,' Bart said. He grabbed his mobile phone and walked towards the back door.

Lara seized the opportunity to appeal to Cam, 'Quick Cam, untie me and let me go. I don't know anything. I was only in the shed because I heard a noise and then got locked in. I don't know what Bart's on about honestly. You know that Curtis will not stop until he finds out where I am.' She hoped to appeal to his sensible side.

'Jesus Lara why were you even here snooping around? There is no way Bart is going to let you go. You know too much,' he looked around desperately in case Curtis should walk through the door at any minute.

'Come on Cam, just let me go please. I won't say anything,' she begged.

'Sure you won't say anything, you stupid girl,' said Bart, back from his phone conversation. He reached over and pushed a dirty white rag over her mouth and nose.

As she inhaled, Lara felt her head become groggy and foggy, her toes started to get pins and needles and the last thing she remembered was Cam looking at her, shaking his head sadly.

27

Chapter Twenty-seven

Curtis opened up the rusty old filing cabinet and put the files he had been working on away. He shook his head slowly, thinking about all the holes that were showing up in the Sam Wilson case. Barrington kept dismissing his concerns, telling him patronisingly that his source was watertight. It just didn't make any sense. Sam Wilson was out of town and on the road for many of the dates that the snowdropper had struck. *Why then does Barrington insist that it's Wilson? Of course, there was the evidence of the underwear found on the property which couldn't be disputed. Unless... No, that would be ridiculous. Get a grip man.* Curtis thought, biting his thumbnail. *I'm going to get a nosebleed with all this to-ing and fro-ing,* he thought. Just as suddenly his mind went to Lara and the amazing night they had spent together. With a shy smile of re-membrance, it was all he could do to stop himself from running out the door to her place and throwing his arms around her. He just couldn't believe how lucky he was to have spent such a special night with her and he hoped it would be one of many. No, not just one of many, but the start of a serious relationship. He didn't dare to say the word out loud but what he felt for Lara was definitely not a one-night stand. From the moment he had clapped eyes on her in the little car after the roo inci-dent he had been intrigued. He couldn't deny that she was extremely good looking with her tall and willowy figure, straight long brown hair and brilliant blue eyes. But it was more than her good looks; it was her sunny, calming and quiet personality that had won him over. After that first kiss under the full moon, he had been biding his time till he could ask her out, but what happened last night was beyond his wildest dreams. Even though there was a lot of stuff going on in his work life, he still managed to smile every time he thought about Lara and their magical night together.

When the door opened Sam Wilson and his lawyer came out. He had been given bail and was now free to go and pick up his boys from Marg's. Curtis grabbed his car keys as he had promised Sam that he would drive him to Marg's and also take him and the boy's home to their property.

As they got in the police cruiser Sam turned to him, 'I absolutely swear to you Curtis, I didn't take anyone's underwear, and I don't know how they got in my shed. And I absolutely don't know why this has happened to me. Yes, I admit I was stupid where Bill is concerned. I just didn't know what to do with him so I left him home all day watching TV. When my wife passed, I think I was in such a state that nothing really made any sense to me. I was floundering man. I know there's no excuse, but that Marg lady said he can actually go to the primary school with Tom. I had no idea that he could do that.' Sam scraped his hand through his thick hair. 'After my wife died I kind of went into a slump. She was the one that dealt with all the school and kid stuff while I was out earning a living. Listen mate, I know it's all gone to shite but I regret it all now. Nora would be rolling in her grave if she could see what a mess I've made of it.'

'I dunno Sam, I believe you but we have to work out how the evidence got in your shed,' said Curtis, with a rise of his shoulders. As they got to Marg's he pulled the police car to the curb and turned to look at Sam. 'You've come to a town where we look after our own and if you do the right thing by the town, they will look after you. Marg's going to sort all the school stuff out for Bill so don't stress too much. Go in there and give your boys a big hug. I'm sure they are confused and miss you like crazy.'

Sam said, 'You know I didn't randomly pick this town. I thought my birth mother lived here but it turns out I was wrong.' His mouth formed a sad line.

'What do you mean mate?' replied Curtis.

'Before she died, my adoptive mother told me my birth mother's name and where she had moved to after she left her family home. Apparently, an aunty of hers kept in contact with my adoptive parents. Her name was Dorothea Maxwell, but there was no record of her ever living here when I went to the council building.'

'I'm sorry Sam, I've not heard of any Maxwell's ever living here; or of a Dorothea, or even a Dot for that matter.'

'Never mind, it was a fool's errand anyway. As if my birth mother would even want to know me anyway, look at the bloody mess I've made of things,' he wiped a hand across his face, sighing heavily.

Curtis followed Sam into Marg's home where the two boys came screaming down the hallway yelling for their dad. *He just seems like such a decent guy and a good dad, even though he should never have left Bill alone like that,* thought Curtis as he witnessed the boys jumping into their fathers embrace. He wondered if he would ever be lucky enough to have two sons, well maybe a son and daughter, he smiled at the scene in front of him.

28

Chapter Twenty-eight

The two boys jumped into the back of the police cruiser with their dad. When they got out of town Curtis put on the siren and he thought Bill was going to blow a gasket with excitement. He kept saying, 'Do it again. Do it again,' clapping his hands together.

When he had driven the Wilson's home Curtis turned back towards town. He couldn't wait to see Lara again and put his foot on the accelerator, being careful not to exceed the speed limit in his excitement. He pulled up outside her place, half expecting her to be waiting on the balcony. He took the stairs two at a time and knocked on her door. There was no answer. *That's strange where is she?* he thought. He picked up her mobile from the wrought iron table and noticed her cold, half-drunk tea. He went down to the cafe half expecting her to be sitting at the bench talking to Janie, who he found unpacking the last of the lunch dishes from the dishwasher. 'Hey, Janie how are you? Have you seen Lara?' He sat down at the counter and picked up one of her muffins from the cake stand.

'Hey you, no I haven't since I was with you yesterday. What's going on with the Wilsons?' she grabbed a plate and slid it under his muffin to try and catch the crumbs.

'Sam's out on bail and I've just dropped them all back at their place. I don't know Janie; the evidence is there but it all feels a bit off somehow.'

'What do you mean Curtis?' she asked, raising her eyebrows.

'I don't know, he just doesn't seem like the type and he has emphatically told me that he didn't do it. I kind of believe him but then there's the evidence,' he shook his head.

'Well evidence can be planted, you know,' she replied.

'Okay but by who and why. That's the twenty-million-dollar question here,' he said.

'It's your job to figure that out,' she reached over and gave his arm a little squeeze.

Later that night when Janie and Curtis were having dinner he said, 'Where could Lara be? Her phone and half-drunk cup of tea are still upstairs on the balcony. It's so weird that she would just leave like that.' When she hadn't come home after dinner Curtis really started to worry. 'I think I'm going to go for a walk and see if anyone has sighted her. I've rung Des and he said she left straight after the meeting he had had with Marg. So, I don't know where she could be.' He rose from the kitchen table and took his dishes over to the dishwasher.

'You seem awfully invested for a friend. She could be out having a drink with someone, or she could be out for dinner,' Janie said, giving her brother a long searching look.

'You're right but my gut tells me differently. I really don't think she would just leave her phone sitting on the outdoor table,' he replied over his shoulder, while walking toward the front door, not quite ready yet to confess to Janie that they were actually more than friends.

'Well let me know if there's anything I can do,' she yelled after him as the door swung closed.

He made his way along the street until he got to the Pub. He had a quick look inside but couldn't see her anywhere. Pearl and Shirl were having dinner at one of the corner tables.

'Sorry to interrupt your dinner ladies but have either of you seen Lara this afternoon?' he asked, standing behind them.

'No pet I haven't seen hide nor hair of her,' said Pearl, turning to look at him. 'But Shirl, you said you saw her earlier.'

'Yes, she was heading down the alleyway between our shop and the Olsen's. She looked to be in a frightful hurry, running like the clappers. I called out but she didn't hear me,' said Shirl, picking up her knife and fork and tucking into her Mexican Parma.

'Why Curtis, what's happened to Lara?' asked Pearl.

'Oh, it's nothing ladies but if you do see her can you give me a quick text. Enjoy your dinner,' he said, turning towards the door.

Pearl and Shirl yelled out 'Hoo roo,' after him and continued with their meal.

Just as he was about to go through the front door, Curtis caught the figure of Josh coming into the bar. He moved towards him. 'What exactly is your reason for still being here mate? Lara has made it perfectly clear she doesn't want you hanging around,' he said, with menace in his voice.

Josh turned around with a sneer on his face. 'That would be none of your business *mate*. If I choose to stay in this one-horse town then that's my business and nothing to do with you.' He turned to the bar and called Paddy over with a wave of his hand.

Curtis held his hands at his sides, just staring at the back of his head. He flexed his fists once, then twice, wondering again why this guy just didn't leave town. Could he have something to do with why Lara is missing? He didn't think so but couldn't ignore it just yet. Paddy poured Josh a beer and then looked at Curtis with a raised eyebrow and a nod of his head to see if he wanted a beer as well.

'I'm all good thanks Paddy. Have you seen Lara around today?'

'Nah sorry mate I haven't seen her since the dinner party,' he said, moving along the bar to serve another customer.

'Look, tell me, have you seen Lara today?' Curtis demanded of Josh. He hated the fact that he was still speaking to the man who had hurt Lara.

'No, I haven't seen her. Why?' he asked suspiciously, again turning towards Curtis and looking him in the eye.

'She's gone missing so if you've done anything to her, I tell you...' A muscle twitched in Curtis's cheek as he clamped his teeth together.

'Missing? How long?' he asked, seeming to take Curtis a bit more seriously.

'Since she came home from work,' he said, realising how weak that sounded. It was only really two hours.

'Well come and find me when it's been twenty-four hours. What sort of cop are you?' he sniggered and turned his back, dismissing Curtis.

In a cloud of frustration Curtis left the pub and crossed the street towards the IGA. When he got to the alleyway, he headed down it towards the back carpark. It was starting to get dark and he wished he'd thought about bringing a torch but it was too late now. He grabbed his phone and turned on the light to have a quick look around the path. Nothing caught his attention. When he got to the back car park there were no cars or people around. *What the hell was she doing here?* he thought, as he walked past the back of the IGA. He noticed the green shed but it was padlocked so he went on past the Olsen Brothers store and ended up at the outskirts of the city centre. Still, he found no sign of Lara or any clues to be had. He turned and headed back to her place hoping she had returned safe and sound.

He waited on her outdoor setting, sitting next to her half-drunk tea and mobile phone. When she hadn't arrived home by midnight he really started to worry. As he looked out onto the street, he heard the sound of a semi-trailer coming down the main road with its lights off. He quickly memorized its number plate as it went by the streetlight, but couldn't get a good look at the driver. It was one of the Olsen trucks. *Why is it leaving so late and with its lights off,* he thought, *this has to be the truck that Lara had seen all those months ago with the hoodie guy?* He contemplated getting in his ute and following the truck but didn't think that would really get him anywhere. No, he was best to get some sleep and then start the search properly tomorrow if Lara still hadn't shown up.

There was nothing else for him to do, so he went home to bed and tried to get some shut eye before his shift started tomorrow. He tossed and turned all night, thinking about different scenarios of where Lara could be. Everything kept coming back to the Olsen's and that semi-trailer. At three o'clock in the morning he was kicking himself that he didn't follow it. His mind went to some dark places and he wished like hell that when the morning came, Lara would be standing on her balcony with her sunny smile, laughing at his worry.

When morning finally arrived, he quickly showered, dressed, and headed once again to Lara's. He knocked on her door again and then tried Lara's handle, surprised when it opened on the first go. *So, she left but didn't lock her door... Interesting.* Her place was deserted but there was evidence that she had been preparing dinner; she had taken enough chicken for two from the freezer, and there was a bottle of their favourite Pinot Grigio, now warm, and two glasses on the bench. *She was definitely not planning on going anywhere,* he thought. When he got to work, he stormed into Barrington's office and told him his concerns.

'What do you mean she's gone missing? It hasn't even been twelve hours. She's probably shacked up with someone for all you know. You seem to be taking this pretty damn personally, Gold.'

Curtis stormed from Barrington's office, ignoring his sergeant's barking after him to come back in and talk about it reasonably. Curtis couldn't explain it, but he had the sick feeling in his stomach that something had happened to Lara and it was all to do with the Olsen's. He rang Des, and when the school principal answered and told him that Lara hadn't shown up for work his fears were confirmed. There was absolutely no way that Lara would not show up to her work without calling; something was seriously wrong. He jumped in his ute and headed towards Talbot where one of his best mates and the son of his old sergeant worked as a detective. For some reason, his gut told him not to trust Barrington.

29

Chapter Twenty-nine

When Lara woke, she was in a dark, confined space. Her arms and legs were bound in a thick scratchy rope that burnt her sensitive skin when she tried to move. The air smelt of old musty boots. When she swallowed, there was a metallic taste at the back of her throat that made her gag. She was thirsty and her head pounded. *What the hell,* she thought. In her muddled mind, she tried to gather herself, *take deep breaths, breathe...* But every time she inhaled, she smelt the foul air. She breathed as shallowly as possible and hoped it would filter the air somehow. *Take stock Lara....* The last thing she remembered was following the hoodie man down the laneway and then bang she was here. *Wait,* she remembered there was a shed and truck and yes, *Bart Olsen! The bloody bastard drugged me.*

As Lara turned her head from left to right, she thought she was in a kind of boot, but noticed it was slightly bigger and lighter; it was a small rectangular area. She felt around on the floor, there was a thin mattress underneath her. She could see the roof was lined like the inside of a car, and to her left there was what looked like a black curtain. She tried to move it with her head but just couldn't manage to find the opening. On both ends there were dirty blacked out windows about the size of a small laptop. That was how the small amount of dappled light was getting in. She felt around on the floor with her fingertips, hoping to find something to help her escape but all she felt was rags of material everywhere. It was hard going with her arms bound. She managed to pull one around to her side and in the shallow light she could make out the lace of someone's underwear. *Jesus, the snowdropper...* But that didn't make sense. *Why would Bart Olsen go to all this trouble to kidnap her over ladies' underwear? What, are they running a second-hand underwear business?* No, there was way more going on here and Lara knew that she was in serious trouble. Bart knew, or thought he knew, that Lara had stumbled onto something sinister that was going on in that back shed and the truck. She also remembered Bart mentioning the Wolf Pack which sent a small shiver down her spine. *Ahh,* she had an epiphany... *I'm in that sleeping part at the back of the truck where the long-haul drivers sleep. So that means the hoodie guy is our snowdropper and that was why Barrington was warning Olsen to tell him to stop. But what are they up to? It must be something bad for them to go to the trouble of kidnapping me. God Goldie, I need you please come and save me,* she willed her thoughts to travel across the universe to prick at the corners of Curtis's mind.

She tried to work out how long she had been out of action. She had her watch on but there was no way she could see it from behind her back. She tried to manipulate the binds on her wrists but every time she did, they bit further into her skin. *Come up with a plan Lara,* she thought. For her whole adult life, Lara had loved reading romance and mystery novels. *What would the heroine Lacey Johnson from 'The Rain falls' do? Would she wait for the gorgeous Detective Nicolas Bonaparte to come and rescue her, or would she kick butt herself and break out of the situation that she found herself in? Lacey would definitely kick butt! I am so not going to go down without a fight, not after finding Curtis and my wonderful job and River Bend and my new friends. Lara, think.* She began investigating the small area again, but this time with a determination that it was not going to be her coffin and that there would be some way to escape. Suddenly, her fingertips touched something hard and cold. She felt what seemed to be a screwdriver or a wrench of some sort. Lara pulled it towards her body with her fingertips and tried to manipulate it under the rope, but it kept falling from her grasp. Her arms and legs ached from being in the one position for so long, but she was determined to escape. She sat up with her knees flush against her torso and arched her butt upwards pulling her tied arms under her legs. She nearly gave up as a lone tear wound down her cheek getting caught in the fine lines around her mouth. She shook her head and with steely determination she tried something different. She pushed her body back and pulled her arms forward until she could push her arms under her legs and *viola* her arms were in front of her. *Definitely helps to have gone to gymnastic classes for ten years.* She quickly tried to undo her leg binds with the tips of her fingers and managed to get her pointer finger under the knot and loosen it. When her feet were free, she went for the screwdriver only to discover that it was a file. *Don't give up now Lara you've got this,* she thought, as she placed the tool between her knees and sawed her binding back and forth. After about ten minutes the rope started to give, and she managed to untie the knot. She cried out just as the binds broke realising that she was free.

Rubbing her sore wrists, she hesitantly poked her head around the black curtain that blocked the window. The cabin was empty except for disregarded Macca's and takeaway containers and drink cups. Lara unlatched the sliding glass and slipped out onto the double cab seat landing on the trash. She looked to be in a service lane on the side of a freeway. The sunlight hurt her eyes after being in the blackened-out cab. *Where the hell is hoodie guy and the Olsen's?* She prised open the door and climbed down as quietly as she could, nearly falling onto the asphalt as her knees buckled from under her. The area seemed to be deserted. In the distance, Lara heard motor bikes heading down the freeway. All of her instincts told her to hide. She ran as quickly as her aching and stiff legs would carry her and hid behind a large crop of lantana bushes by the side of the service lane. From her position she made out four motorbikes, maybe Harleys, she wasn't a bike connoisseur, come into the area and park by the truck. These bikers did not look friendly. They had on the full gear, black leathers, and long wiry beards. *Jeez it's the Wolf Pack,* she recognised one of the bikers from the pub as he took off his helmet and headed towards the truck.

'The idiots left the door open.' She heard him say to his gang as he climbed into the cab. 'Shit there's no one here,' he said, in a graveling sounding voice.

'What the fuck! Olsen said the girl was tied up in the back. Search the back of the truck,' said another biker with a tattooed face.

'Hey Fender, there's some cut rope here, I think she's done a runner. Either that, or that idiot driver has her,' said the biker who had climbed into the cab looking for her.

Lara knew that she only had one shot. Very quietly she snuck into the bush and when she thought she was far enough away, she ran using the cover of the thick eucalyptus trees to protect and hide her. She didn't stop for at least half an hour when she crouched down by an old ghost gum and breathed heavily, listening for the sounds of anyone following her. All was silent. Taking in some deep breaths, Lara took stock of her situation. *I have to find help,* she thought, *but I have to be careful as those bikies are probably searching for me.* Lara checked her watch; it was five o'clock in the afternoon. It would be dark soon.

She walked on using the mellow light of the moon to guide her. She tripped over a gnarly root and came down heavily on her knee. She felt the sting of broken skin and the prick of tears in her eyes. Her hands and wrists still ached from the rope burn and she knew that she had to find water quickly if she was to survive being out here. She stopped to listen to her surroundings, hoping to at least hear a car or something, anything but alas there was nothing that suggested human help. A barn owl hooted in the tree above her when she realised that she had to stop and rest or else she was never going to make it out of the bush. In her muddled mind she thought she could hear the sound of running water. She pushed past a group of spinifex bushes to find a small creek that flowed into a kind of catchment. There were thick green weeds growing around the bank and the outline of a native duck swimming lazily on the muddy water was just visible by the light of the moon. *Thank*

God, she thought as she leant down and cupped her hands to drink the lifesaving liquid. It tasted of mud, but it was all she had for now. When she'd had her fill, she found a mound of grass by an old ghost gum and tried to make a safe haven for herself. She was just lucky that it was the start of autumn and the frosts hadn't set in yet.

As she sat there swatting away mozzies, the tears started to well in her eyes. She desperately wanted Goldie. His strong body would protect her now. His soft words would calm her. *Why had she waited so long to be with him? Would the Olsen brothers find her? Would the bikies find her first? Which would be worse?* She shuddered in the cool evening light. She realised she was in a terrible situation. Even worse than the awful Covid times. Back then it had been only Josh she was frightened of, now it was all the people trying to hurt her, as well as, the environment she found herself in. Lara's mind drifted to that terrible night when Josh had come home from work in one of his moods. She'd had his dinner in the fridge ready to heat and when she'd taken it out of the Glad Wrap, he'd criticized her for not waiting to eat with him. She knew that telling him it was ten o'clock at night was not going to help her cause. She quickly microwaved the dinner and placed it on the table in front of him. But when he bit into it, he spat it out and yelled for a glass of water. 'You stupid bitch, are you trying to burn me now,' he yelled angrily. In one swoop he knocked the plate, knife, and fork off the table, causing them to crash onto the tiled floor. The cracked dinner ware mingled with the spilled peas, potato, and meat. When Josh stood, he toppled the table over as well, just to add to the carnage.

Lara cowered in the corner waiting for the blows to come but instead Josh picked up the steak knife and came menacingly towards her. His face had turned a purple colour and his lips were snarled over his bared teeth. He took a step closer, raising the knife above his head as if he were going to thrust it down into her body. At that moment flight or fight came over Lara and she jumped up, pushing him backwards into the upturned table, the sound of the crash echoing around the room. She ran for the door, hearing him calling her name from the kitchen but she took off down the hallway and thanked God that her bag was sitting on the hall stand just by the front door. It was a plan of Lara's to always have it there in case she had to get out in a hurry. She grabbed her bag and ran to her car, fumbling for her keys with shaking hands. Once in the relative safety of the little Pulsar, she'd taken off to her mum and dad's place. At one point she had to pull over as she was shaking so much that her hands could not hold the steering wheel properly. It hadn't quite hit her yet, but she knew in her heart that Josh had been going to stab her. No matter what happened she resolved that she would never, ever go back to that house and to that man. If the cops pulled her over for being out of curfew, she would demand to see a female policewoman and explain her domestic situation.

As she lay by the old gum tree she shivered at the terrible memory, but Lara also felt proud of herself. She had survived domestic violence and had lived to tell the tale. She was so used to putting herself down over Josh and their relationship that it was a totally cathartic feeling laying there in the dark, realising that it wasn't actually her fault. The only thing she did wrong was to trust that toxic man. She was strong enough to escape him using her education as a means of getting out of Melbourne. But even that let her down as he followed her anyway. She was determined that when she got home, if she got home, she was going to apply for an intervention order against Josh because she would never ever be put in a situation like that again. Now she had to be strong enough to get back to Goldie, a man who would never hurt her, a man who understood domestic violence at its very core.

She heard a rustling in the bushes beside her and yelled out in fright as a creature of some type ran off through the bush. Now it was pitch black, even the moon had let her down as it crept behind some dark clouds. The night noises of the bush surrounded her; the hoot of an owl, a call and snarl of a ringtail possum, it was like a different world at night. She missed the daytime sounds of River Bend. She looked up at the stars. They truly were beautiful, but she didn't have the luxury of enjoying them as her eyelids slowly started to droop. Sleep came in fits and fads.

30

Chapter Thirty

Jason Perry, Curtis's best mate from the academy, opened his laptop to type in his password and said, 'Jesus Goldie what the hell was Lara doing hanging around with those losers?'

'Well, she wasn't hanging with them, but the laneway near the IGA was the last time she was sighted. I've got such a bad feeling about this Jase. You have to be able to help. Bloody Barrington is hopeless and I don't feel I can trust him anymore.'

'Good for you because, and you can't tell anyone this yet, the department has had eyes on the Olsen's for a few weeks now. We have eyes on the ground in River Bend and just between you and me, Barrington is also being investigated for having links with criminals.'

'Jeez you're kidding me? No wait, that doesn't surprise me, he has been acting extremely weird lately. Tell me what you know so far?' Curtis sat down at the kitchen table opposite Jase.

'When Bart Olsen was living in Melbourne, he was one of the key members of an outlaw motorcycle club called the Wolf Pack.' Curtis nodded his head knowing all about the Wolf Pack and their attachment to the Olsen's. Jase continued, 'They were known for extortion and drug running. Do you know all those tobacco stores that got burnt down in Melbourne?' He waited for Curtis to nod his understanding before continuing, 'Well that was them, but we had no solid evidence to convict anyone. We put in an undercover narc and that's how we have been getting all our intel. We knew that there was someone on the inside and we were ninety percent sure that it was Barrington. In fact, I have a hunch that my father discovered the dodgy goings on when old man Olsen was still alive, way before the brothers arrived. I reckon my dad was killed for having that knowledge and then they managed to worm Barrington in somehow. You have to understand that this is a multi-million dollar outfit with some very nasty characters at the helm. You know I never believed that Dad committed suicide. It just never sat well with me. I knew my father; he was not the type. All that bull about him having depression after mum died, nope not having a bar of it. So, when I heard about this investigation, I was right onto it and put my name forward for the assignment. Our inside man says not only are they moving vapes but they have started running a heroin ring out of the hardware store as well. They hide it in trucks and drive it across the border in pellets of feed and stuff to NSW.'

'Oh yeah,' Curtis interrupted, 'Lara saw a semi leave River Bend a few months ago and I witnessed one last night. God, I could kick myself that I didn't bloody follow it. They must be leaving with the drugs in the middle of the night.' He was convinced that they had both witnessed the drug run.

'Our man got news early this morning that a girl was kidnapped because she was discovered at the shed where the drugs were being kept. I am assuming that's Lara.'

'Bloody Hell Jase, tell me you know where she is?' he almost begged his mate.

'The last we heard she was in the back of a truck going over the border and it was meant to be met by some really seedy members of the Wolf Pack. But, and this is her good luck, it seems that when they got to the truck it was empty. Now our guy doesn't know what's happened to her or the driver of the semi who's also disappeared.'

'This story just keeps getting worse.' Curtis pushed his hands together to stop them from shaking in anger.

'I have sent in ground crew to search the truck and try and work out what's happened to Lara. But Curtis, it actually does get worse. I've just been informed by command that there is an out-of-control bushfire in the area,' he said, just as his phone beeped.

Curtis could hear him talking to a man on the other end of the line.

'Yeah, okay that's great news thanks mate. I'll jump in the car and meet you out there,' he said, as he hung up from the caller.

'They've found Lara?' said Curtis, with hope in his voice.

'Nah not yet unfortunately. But they have found what looks like illegal vapes in the back of the truck and they are sending the dog squad in to check for drugs. There is evidence that Lara was there and, this is strange, they discovered a pile of ladies lingerie in the sleeping compartment.'

'The bloody snow dropper,' said Curtis.

'Snowdropper! Fill me in on the way; I'm about to head out there if you want to come along for the ride. I've sent my man in River Bend with a team to arrest the Olsen's. At this stage Barrington doesn't know we are on to him. I am going to enjoy taking that bastard down.'

Curtis and Jase jumped into his police vehicle and headed towards the NSW border.

31

Chapter Thirty-one

Lara woke up with a start. *What was that?* she thought as the sound of rustling could be heard from behind her. She witnessed a kangaroo and its joey hop off through the bush, their long tails whipping the spinifex grass as they glided past. The sun was beginning to rise, turning the bush a spectacular red colour that one can only really witness in the early morning light. The welts on her legs caused by the mozzies or ants, she had no idea what, itched and she pushed a cross into them with her thumb nail. This was an old wives' tale her family always swore by to stop the itch. She slowly got up and made her way to the stream and doused her face in the cool muddy water. The water mixed with her tears. *Stop it Lara,* she chastised herself for being weak. She cupped the water and rubbed it on her arms and around the chafing on her wrists and ankles. Suddenly she sniffed the air. *What's that?* she thought, *it smells like smoke!* Just then through the bush, a mob of kangaroos bounced past heading towards the open scrub lands. She had to push herself up against a tree to stop them from knocking her over. Cockatoos screeched in the nearby trees like a fire siren going off, warning the surrounding animals of present danger. The bush came alive. It was almost an electric feeling, the atmosphere had changed from calm to panic. From the scrub a small echidna waddled towards the bank and started to bury itself in the mud. *Think Lara,* she thought to herself, *do I run or wade into the stream? God Goldie, where are you, I need you?*

Lara could hear the fire getting closer. It sounded like a jet engine moving through the bush. She really didn't think that she could outrun it so she waded into the cool waters of the gushing stream. Like the little echidna she started to rub the cool mud over her exposed arms and face. She waded right into the middle of the stream and made her way to the deeper catchment area furthest away from the bank. The water came just up to her neck. Quickly she took off her t-shirt and put it over her face.

She could now see the fire coming towards her through the trees. It was a dirty deep red, and like a monster it seemed to be eating up everything in its path. Big puffs of black smoke were rising up above it into the clear blue sky, mixing in streaks of grey and white amongst the blue. Instantly the air seemed to have all the moisture and oxygen sucked out of it. Black ash fell from above onto her wet t-shirt, hitting it with a sizzle. It was literally raining ash. Animals waded into the stream to hide in its life-saving water. A goanna swam past her but seemed more interested in getting to the other side of the stream than investigating the human. The fire hit a nearby tree and in an astonishing way travelled up the trunk and exploded into the oil of the eucalyptus leaves, bursting into the sky. The tops of the trees looked like burning torches. The ball of fire skipped from tree to tree until the canopies resembled a ring of burning fire.

Suddenly the fire jumped the stream and the trees on the other side of the bank caught. Burnt koalas dropped from the branches and Lara screamed out in fright and horror as she saw a mother and baby on fire, fall to the ground with a thud. The air was thick with smoke. Lara lay deeper in the stream and tried to breathe through the cotton of her t-shirt. The water temperature heated up but was bearable and Lara knew she had made the right decision staying put; the fire was like a raging bull tearing through all in its path. Through the intensity of the heat, she felt the skin on her face start to burn and blister. She held her breath and dunked under the water giving her skin some relief. When she came up for air she was surrounded by a thick grey smoke drifting off the surface of the water like fog. She pushed the wet t-shirt over her mouth and tried to get in a decent breath, but it made her cough as she breathed in the toxic air.

Just when she thought she was going to be found dead and drowned in this muddy hell hole the fire moved on. The smoke haze thinned out and she could just make out the outline of the burnt eucalyptus trees on the bank. Through the smoke, she could see small spot fires amongst the debris of the forest but the worst of it seemed to have passed. She took the t-shirt off her face and looked around at the devastation that surrounded her. *God that was close.* She sobbed, shaking uncontrollably in the warm water, as the realisation of what she had been through and witnessed hit her. She let out a final shuddering sob and made her way over to the bank where she lay down at the edge of the water trying to calm her nerves. The little echidna started to scratch his way out of the mud. She cried in relief, knowing that they had both survived the wild-fire.

32

Chapter Thirty-two

Curtis and Jase raced towards the site of the abandoned semi. On the radio they heard updates about the bush fire that was devastating the area. The whole south side was being evacuated and the boys could see the cars and caravans heading away from the fire on the other side of the road. Only themselves and emergency services were silly enough to be heading towards the disaster.

'We have a team at the truck site transporting the drugs that the dogs sniffed out to head office, plus it looks like there are hundreds of illegal vapes stuffed in boxes, as well. They have also sent a tow truck to take the semi away for forensics to gather evidence. Luckily there was that wind change and it has all escaped the fire or we would be in a whole lot of trouble.' Jase told Curtis as he slowed down to let an emergency vehicle pass him safely.

'Still nothing on Lara? Where the hell is she?' replied a very worried Curtis.

'Nothing yet mate but we have the emergency services looking for her. It's just a bit tricky because of this damn fire. A team from River Bend and Talbot are heading towards the area and they will also be searching for her. She is our absolute priority Curtis, I promise mate. Now tell me about this snowdropper.'

'It started about six months ago. Random underwear went missing from random people's homes. We just never had enough evidence to convict anyone until Barrington got wind that one of the new locals was involved. And of course, when he went to the farm house there was evidence in the shed of ladies' undies and bras. Barrington arrested him but it all felt off to me. The guy, a father of one of Lara's school kids, didn't fit the profile and was also away trucking for many of the break-ins. But Barrington insisted. Now it looks like it could be a massive setup.'

They arrived at the site just in time to see the tow truck with the semi attached to the back head off towards Melbourne. A marquee had been set up where the State Emergency Service volunteers were milling around looking at maps. There was a sea of orange as volunteers from River Bend and Talbot gathered to protect their countryside. They made their way over to the tent to find out the latest information. The man in charge came over to them and showed them the areas that they had already searched.

'The fire has already burnt out in the scrublands so I've sent your guys from River Bend back along the waterway to search for survivors; I am just about to get this lot to go further west as one of the police helicopters has sighted a body near the river,' said the commander of the local SES, pointing to the map he had in his hands.

'God no. What can we do?' asked Curtis, pulling his hand through his hair and feeling sick to his stomach. *Please, please, please don't let it be Lara,* he silently prayed. He couldn't lose her now that he had just found her.

'Come with us, we need all the help we can get. There are still spot fires so grab some overalls from the tent and get ready to meet us here in about ten minutes.'

Finally, Curtis felt like he was doing something productive. He still didn't understand how he could have missed the whole Olsen thing and was kicking himself for not being more protective of Lara. *If they have hurt her in any way, I'll bloody kill them. If this body is Lara's... God, I don't know what I'll do. No, it just can't be Lara,* he nearly sobbed out loud as he pulled on a pair of orange overalls.

They joined the crew and started walking through the burnt and scarred bush. In parts it was as black as night where the fire had devastated the environment. His arm brushed against a burnt-out tree and a black smear of soot appeared on his overalls. He just couldn't imagine anyone surviving out here, especially a city girl like Lara who had never experienced all the Aussie bush had in store. There were burnt carcasses of small animals that hadn't managed to outrun the wildfire everywhere. Crows and other scavenger birds circled around, landing on the bodies for a tasty feed. Curtis had to forcefully push away the image of the body up west having similar birds picking from its flesh. It made him sick to the core and the smoke or, maybe it was his emotions, made his eyes sting and water. He wiped the tears away and put his head down so that Jase couldn't see how upset he was.

The SES crew put out the spot fires as Curtis and Jase called out Lara's name. It was like she had disappeared completely after leaving the semi. *Where the hell are you, Lara? Please don't be this body.* A shiver went down his spine and bile rose up in his throat.

At that moment one of the radios kicked into life. 'We've found her. We will need an ambulance to meet us at the rest stop. Repeat an ambulance to meet us at the rest stop,' echoed the person on the other end. Curtis's heart turned to stone. He felt sick to his stomach. *My poor Lara,* he almost cried, but he knew that he had to be strong for her sake.

Curtis and Jase turned back around so that they could be waiting when the ambulance and Lara arrived.

33

Chapter Thirty-three

She felt herself being gently lifted up into strong arms. *Goldie,* she thought with a sigh of relief. He had found her. She knew in her heart of hearts that he would be the one to rescue her. She put her tired and scalded arms around his strong neck and nuzzled into that spot she loved, just below his chiselled jaw. Her eyes gently drooped and for the first time in a long time she felt safe. As they came out of the clearing, she could hear the sound of sirens in the background, cutting through the quietness of the bush. It was all gone. It was all destroyed by the bushfire. She nuzzled closer into Curtis, but something felt wrong. Something felt off; familiar, but different. Slowly she opened her eyes and with a jolt in her foggy smoke-filled mind, she recognised her rescuer.

'What the hell are you doing?' came a male voice from behind her. She heard bits and pieces of heated conversation going back and forth until her mind became a whirl of confusion. She held on closer to the person who had rescued her from the fire, terrified of the Olsen brothers or the bikies finding her. Then she blacked out.

When she regained consciousness, the first thing she noticed was the white ceiling above her head. Where was she? This was not her apartment; the ceiling there was a cream colour with a ceiling rose and a wrought iron light above her bed thanks to Janie's wonderful taste. Lara's whole body ached. She heard an annoying beeping noise beside her and slowly moved her head to see what it was. Beside her bed there was a drip of some sort and she realised that she had tubes coming from her arms. It was then that it all came crashing back down on her.

'Lara, you're awake?' said a male voice, from the other side of the bed.

She hesitantly turned her head to look.

'Josh?' she said in confusion. *What was Josh doing here?*

'Oh my God Lars, you had me so worried,' he said. He got up off the chair and gingerly held her left hand, as though he didn't want to disturb the bandages. She didn't get it. What was Josh doing here? As far as she was concerned, he had left River Bend and she was never going to see him again. Yet here he was as if nothing had happened between them. Was she going mad?

'When I found you down by the river, I honestly thought I had lost you. I couldn't believe it when I discovered that you were alive,' he said, wiping a tear away from his eye.

'It was you who saved me?' she asked in a confused voice.

'Yes of course it was me, I had been searching for you. When I heard you were kidnapped by the Olsen's I just couldn't believe it Lars. You mean everything to me,' he said with a sob, bringing his head down close to hers, kissing her on the lips gently. She kissed him back not knowing what else to do.

Clearly, she had been hit on the head because she was sure she had ended things with Josh, but he was acting as if nothing untoward had happened between them. Just like that she remembered Curtis and slowly but firmly placed her right hand on his chest and pushed him away from her. She felt a jolt of pain move up her arm at the physical movement.

'What are you doing Josh? I am really grateful that you rescued me, but we are definitely not together. I am with Curtis.'

'We can give it another go Lars,' he begged. 'I'll do better this time.'

'For God's sake get it through your head, I am with Curtis. You missed out Josh. I will forgive you for the way you treated me, but I will not forget. So, I am telling you to leave now, and if you don't, I will put in a formal complaint and take out an AVO on you which won't look good for your career,' she said, and slumped back on her pillow exhausted, but still determined to live by her vow at the waterhole; to never be abused again.

Josh looked at her and it was like a light-bulb moment as he really truthfully understood for the very first time that she meant everything she was saying. He had lost. 'Okay, okay I don't want you getting upset,' he said, in a condescending voice. 'If that's how you really feel then I couldn't really give a shit anymore.' And there he was... The violent, spiteful, Josh she had shared a life with for two excruciating years. 'You aren't worth the stress. Bloody Curtis is welcome to you. I was only here because I was seconded to Talbot and thought we could have some fun for old times' sake, but clearly not.'

'Wait what, seconded? Were you working here, undercover?' she asked, confused.

'Yes Lara, I've been spying on the Olsen's, coming back and forth from Melbourne. That's the reasons I couldn't just jump up and leave this shit town. The department has had their eye on them for quite some time and it all came to a head this week. Unfortunately, nobody thought that you of all people would become involved in the proceedings,' he said, getting up off the chair. 'Anyway, you have nothing to fear anymore from the Olsen's or the Wolf Pack. They will be behind bars for a very long time. So yes, you can thank me for saving your pathetic life.' He walked towards her bed with a menacing look on his face and, typical Josh, had to have the last word. 'You know,' he reached out and held her arm, tightening his grip, leaning in towards her ear and whispered, 'you are nothing and I can't believe you are stupid enough to choose this shit hole of a town and that idiot cop over me.'

At that moment there was a tap on the door and Janie walked in. When she saw what was happening, she rushed over to the bed pushing Josh out of the way. 'Leave her alone you bastard. How dare you touch her?'

Lara couldn't believe the change that had come over Janie. She was like a terrier dog with a bone determined to get Josh away from her. Josh righted himself and leant against the chair standing up to his full height. 'Piss off you stupid bitch.'

And with a sharp sound that reverberated around the hospital room Janie slapped him full across the face. Lara gasped in shock. Josh's reaction was to ball up his fist and raise it as if he was going to punch Janie in the face. She held his gaze and said in a voice full of steel and confidence, 'Go on, I dare you!'

'If you touch one hair on her head Josh, not only will we charge you for assault but I will have you up on charges for those two years of hell you put me through.' Lara sat up pointing a shaky finger at Josh.

'Yeah, and don't think I won't be laying charges as well if you dare to come near me or my friend ever again,' said Janie, standing up to her full height, staring unblinkingly into Josh's eyes and not backing down. Janie moved over to stand by Lara. 'You heard her, dirt bag. Now get out before I call security.' Janie puffed up like a mother hen and put a hand protectively on Lara's shoulder.

'Fuck you two.' Josh sneered at Janie and Lara and pushed over the chair in anger before slamming the door and disappearing into the bowels of the hospital.

Janie bent down and held Lara in a shaky hug, trying not to disturb her bandages or press against any sore parts. She leant her head gently against Lara's shoulder and in a teary voice said, 'Oh Lara, I know that Curtis told you all about our upbringing and what happened to our father and mother. I just couldn't stand to see that man hurt you and be mean to you. Please don't think less of me for reacting so violently. I just don't know what came over me,' Janie sobbed into Lara's crisp white hospital gown.

'Oh my God Janie, you are my hero. Not only did you protect me, but you were Curtis's protector for all those years. You were a baby yourself and look at you now, a survivor of domestic violence just like me.' Lara lovingly smoothed down the dark curls on Janie's head and felt the tears fall down her face and drip onto her sheets as the words she spoke to Janie really sank in. They were both survivors of domestic violence and they had nothing to be ashamed about, ever again.

After a while Janie got up off the bed and straightened the chair that Josh had knocked over on his hurried escape from the room. 'I've got an overnight bag here with some of your clothes and toiletries in it. Oh, and I picked up your phone from your place as well. It's fully charged for you. Your parents have been ringing nonstop and will be here tomorrow. I've booked them into the Rivy Arms. I'll pop the phone by your bed with the charger and put your stuff in the bathroom. If you need anything else, text me and I will drop it off tomorrow,' Janie said, trying to gain some control. She grabbed Lara's makeup bag and opened up the ensuite door to find somewhere to put it.

'You are a lifesaver, thanks so much Janie. I just... I haven't seen Curtis. Is he around anywhere?' she asked.

'What?! He's been hanging around here all morning, I actually thought he'd been in to visit,' she said, looking around the small room as if expecting him to materialize from thin air. 'That's strange... I'll go and see if I can find him for you but I did see him talking to Jase Perry. Maybe he's gone into work?' Janie bent down to give Lara a gentle kiss on the cheek. 'There's also a bevy of friends out there waiting to hear that you are okay. You have really made a mark on this little town, Lara. I hope you realise how loved you are.'

Lara felt herself start to tear up again and the horrible things that Josh had said to her and Janie were pushed to the back of her mind. In the short time she had been in River Bend she could not imagine ever living anywhere else. Marg, Smithy, the Early twins, Des, Paddy, the Zumba ladies, book club and, of course her beautiful little class... What would she do without them all? Then her thoughts turned to the Golds. Janie had really become her best friend in the time she had been at River Bend. Just like that, her mind wandered to Goldie and she thought of those curls and that body, not to mention his kind and caring nature.

Oh, what she wouldn't give to be wrapped in his arms right now! *Where is he?*

She just hoped he hadn't looked through the window and witnessed Josh kissing her. That could be a disaster.

$$34$$

Chapter Thirty-four

Curtis had been pacing the hospital waiting room for what felt like hours. His mind raced as he thought about how close Lara had come to dying.

'Do you want another coffee, Curtis?' asked Marg, as she also paced behind him.

'God, I couldn't drink another cup of hospital coffee, I'm already crawling out of my skin from the last two. Thanks anyway Marg.'

'This waiting game is as long as a wet week,' said Pearl, as she sat on a hard plastic waiting room chair and picked up her crocheting. 'I think Lara's going to love the colours I've chosen,' she said, almost to herself as she put the crochet hook through the pink and purple wool.

Just then Smithy came through the swing doors that led to the ER.

'Good news my friends. They have sent Lara to the ward and she is out of danger. They are rehydrating her, and her lungs seem to be clear. They have given her oxygen but she is fine now. She did have some minor burns, but I think she'll recover nicely,' he said, facing the little group.

Curtis let out a huge breath of relief and pushed his hands through his already unruly curls. He stumbled back onto one of the orange plastic chairs and put his hands over his face, trying not to cry in front of all his friends.

'Oh, Curtis love, you poor thing. It's been such a nerve-wracking time for you,' said a very kind Marg, patting Curtis on the shoulder.

'She's going to be fine pet,' said Pearl, just as the door to the waiting room opened and Tiffany and Patsy came in carrying homemade sandwiches and store-bought cappuccinos for all to share.

Curtis made his way to room twenty-three, nervous to see Lara after her terrible ordeal. He felt responsible for some reason. In reality he knew he wasn't, but he felt he should have protected her more. He stood at the door and looked through the glass window. *What the hell!* There was bloody Josh bent over, kissing his Lara. The bastard. He was just about to push through the door and give Josh a piece of his mind when Jase appeared at the end of the corridor.

'Curtis, I've been looking for you. They are about to arrest Barrington, I thought you'd want to be there,' he turned, expecting Curtis to follow. Curtis turned back to the window just as Lara pushed Josh away. *Good on ya Lars,* he thought with a smile. *That's my girl.*

'Wait up Jase, I'm right behind you,' he said. He raced after Jase and felt his heart lift as he realised Lara was going to be alright.

Barrington was in the house that he lived in as part of the package he received to come to a country town. Made out of sandstone like most of the buildings around it, it was a two bedroom miner's cottage and sat tucked behind the police station. Some of the task force were directed into the station to confiscate Barrington's laptop, computer, and any other evidence they could find to incriminate him in his links with the Olsen's and their dirty business. When Jason Perry and his team barged through the cottage door, they found Barrington in his room hurriedly packing a suitcase with clothes.

'Going somewhere Barrington?' said Jase, as he stood in the doorway peering at the sergeant.

Barrington stood back looking like a deer caught in the headlights. 'What's the meaning of this? How dare you enter my home uninvited. This is outrageous!' Barrington stammered, closing his suitcase lid quickly.

'Senior Sergeant Barrington, you are under arrest for conspiring to commit an offense with the Olsen brothers and the Wolf Pack, known criminals.'

'Hang on a minute,' interrupted Barrington, as he came around the side of his bed to face Perry. 'Are you bloody kidding me? This is a bloody trumped-up charge and what evidence do you have?'

'Well, you know I don't think it is a trumped-up charge Barrington and don't you worry about the evidence there is plenty of it,' Jase said. Two tech guys burst through the door and started unplugging the computer that was sitting on the desk near his window.

'We will need your phone as well Barrington,' hissed Jase, holding out his hand.

'This is ridiculous,' scoffed Barrington, while Jase handcuffed him and took his phone from the desk. After Jase read him his rights, Barrington was led away, but not before he turned to Curtis and said with a sneer, 'Idiot boy, you are going to be very sorry you crossed me.'

'Maybe, maybe not Barrington. Let's just see what these tech guys find and just remember, the Olsen's will sell your soul to the devil if it means a lighter sentence.' A shadow moved across Barrington's eyes as he went physically pale. *Not so smug now,* thought Curtis, slowly shaking his head.

After a phone call from Janie filling him in on Josh and letting him know that Lara was okay and resting at the hospital, he made his way back to the police station. He was surprised to find Jason Perry talking to, of all people, Josh.

'What the hell are you doing here?' Curtis asked, confused by Josh sitting at his desk and filling out paperwork.

'Oh yeah, you didn't know did you mate? I was here working undercover,' sneered Josh, picking up his pen and continuing to fill out papers.

'Do you two know each other?' asked a confused Jase.

'This is the bastard that abused Lara during the lockdown and has been intimidating her while he has been, so called, working here. He also just had a go at my sister so unless you tell me that you are leaving and leaving town for good, I am going to put out an intervention order against you.'

Josh stood up and came towards Curtis in a menacing way.

'Listen here Josh, back down now,' said Jase in a stern voice. 'If I investigate Curtis's allegations and find them to be correct your job as a copper is done and dusted mate. I've very good friends in very high places and I am not scared to pull some strings. If you have anything to hide, if you have abused Lara and Janie, I would advise you to shut up, sit down, finish the paper work and get the hell out of town and don't ever come back. I will be keeping an eye on you just in case you think it's okay to abuse women.'

35

Chapter Thirty-five

Curtis got to the IGA just before closing time. 'G'day Shirl, how's things?' asked Curtis, picking up a bunch of yellow roses from the black bucket at the front of the shop.

'Hiya Curtis. How's our girl? You know the greatest wealth is health, I am praying that Lara gets her health back very soon.'

'Awe thanks Shirl. I'll be sure to tell her, we all know how much Lara loves a good saying.' He gave Shirl ten dollars and headed out the door with a skip in his step. The late afternoon sun peaked through the gum trees on Main Street leaving blotchy shadows on the white concrete pathway. He hadn't seen Lara since she was brought in by the ambulance the day before, he had been stuck at the station filling out reams of paperwork. Not only had they arrested the Olsen brothers and taken Barrington to Melbourne for questioning, but there was a warrant out for the arrest of the truck driver Paul Zammit. When the police searched the cab, they found lots of ladies' underwear and bras. So, there was their town snowdropper. Before he left for the station Curtis put in a call to Sam Wilson to let him know that he was not a suspect anymore and that the investigation would uncover how and by whom the articles of clothing were found at the farm. Of course, Curtis suspected Barrington of having a hand in all that as a way to take the heat off Zammit and the Olsen's. A theory had begun to emerge that Zammit had intentionally lit the bushfire to cover his tracks, he clearly didn't want the Olsen's to come after him. Maybe the kidnapping was too much for him and he wanted an out. He was now wanted for theft, arson, and manslaughter because a farmer's body had been discovered in the aftermath of the fire.

The dots were all starting to join up. The Olsen's had moved their drug ring to River Bend when they inherited the feed and hardware store because the police had been getting too close to them in Melbourne. It turned out that Barrington was in their pocket because he had gambling debts up to his armpits. The tech guys were just investigating exactly how much Barrington owed and there was evidence that the Olsen's had paid some of his debt, of course, making him in debt to them. Apparently, he spent a lot of time online gambling, with the horses, sports betting and poker. Lara had been at the wrong place at the wrong time and who knew what the Wolf Pack would have done to her if they had caught up with her. He felt such a relief that they were all in custody.

As Curtis was walking towards his car to drive to Talbot Memorial, a text came through from Lara, she was home from the hospital. He turned around towards the Cozy, Cup & Wares, desperate to see her. When he knocked on the door Janie answered and let him in. Lara was sitting on the couch drinking a cup of herbal tea. Curtis went over and sat next to her, holding her hand gently. 'You certainly had us all worried, Nancy Drew. I thought you had given up detective work to leave it to the professionals. He brought her hands to his lips, kissing them gently.

'I am definitely hanging up my hat. No more following men down dark alleyways for me,' she laughed hoarsely and started to cough.

'Here's some water Lara.' Janie went to the tap and filled a large glass for her.

'Thanks Janie,' she took the glass in a shaky hand.

Curtis noticed the burn marks on her hand and face and felt his stomach churn as he once again realised how close he was to losing her.

'I think I'll leave the two of you to chat. Pearl and Shirl dropped off a delicious looking chicken pie that should be ready in about fifteen minutes. It's warming in the oven. Curtis, can I rely on you to look after our girl?' asked Janie, reaching over him and giving Lara a kiss on the cheek.

'Thanks that's so sweet of them,' Lara said, wiping a stray tear from her eye.

'At this rate you won't have to shop until next month. Marg, Tiff and Patsy have all dropped off their specialties as well. There's a big bowl of salad and fresh baked bread on the counter,' she winked, walking out the back door.

Finally, alone, Curtis reached for Lara and cupped her chin gently. 'I've been wanting to do this since I left for work two days ago. Who would have thought I would have to wait so long,' he said, staring directly into her blue eyes. She stared back at him, reaching up and touching his stubbly chin with her fingertips and sending a shiver down his backbone. 'Is it alright if I kiss you?' he whispered breathlessly.

'No it's not okay because I'm going to kiss you,' she replied hoarsely, placing her lips on his. He smelt of peppermint and woody spice. She cupped the back of his head, putting her fingers through his dark locks, massaging his scalp.

He moaned into her mouth, pushing his tongue in gently and opening up her mouth even more. But then he pulled back. 'Are you sure you're okay to be doing this Lara? I don't want to hurt you even more,' he searched the depths of her eyes.

'The only thing that would hurt me Goldie, is not having you in my life and not having you kiss me. I couldn't stop thinking about you the whole time I was out there in the scrublands. When the fire came, I just wanted you with me and I honestly thought I would never see you again. I can't tell you how much that scared me. Even more than the Olsen brothers and the damn Wolf Pack.'

She rested her head on his shoulder and he massaged her back, feeling the bones beneath his hands. She seemed to be even thinner than she was two days ago. *What a terrible ordeal she's been through*, he thought, gently wrapping his hands around her and patting her on the back like she was a small child.

'What have you discovered about the whole drug ring? Detective Jason Perry came and visited me yesterday and took my statement. He filled me in on a few bits and pieces, but I'd love to hear the whole story from you, if you are allowed to tell me of course,' she said, leaning back and looking into his eyes.

After Curtis had told Lara all that he had discovered he took the pie out of the oven and dished out the salad. They ate their dinner on the balcony outside. The sun was just starting to set and it left a fresh glow over the gums. The flowers in her pots had turned a deep red colour that matched the setting sun. The birds nesting in the trees next to her balcony took off up Main Street squawking through the air like kamikaze pilots ducking in and out of the native trees. It was almost as though the town was taking a deep inhalation after all the evilness of the Olsen brothers and the Wolf Pack.

Things were going back to normal, just a small Victorian country town getting on with the close of day.

That night, they lay together. Curtis wrapped his strong arms around her loving the feel of her soft body next to him. They had made love passionately, with Curtis being careful not to rest his full weight on her burnt and bruised body. As they lay in the afterglow of their love-making, he'd told her of his fears, that he thought he had lost her just when he had found her. It had brought up so many terrible feelings, he said, like the loss of his mother and his hometown when he and Janie were younger. 'I just honestly don't understand how men can think that they can treat women like that? I look at my father, Josh, the bloody Olsen's, what makes them believe they have the right to treat people, women, like shit?'

She turned around to face him in the darkness. 'I know Goldie, I know. But not everyone is like that, thank God. You, my dad, Smithy, Paddy. The others unfortunately, are the exception to the rule.' He moved his hand over her soft hair, feeling the silky strands between his fingers. She wrapped her arms around him, and snuggled into his chest. He could feel her heart beat and he was finally at peace.

36

Chapter Thirty-six

'Lara lovely, your father and I have been so worried about you. Are you okay? Do you need anything?' said a perplexed Florence Benton to her daughter, who was sitting on the couch in her apartment.

'Mum, I'm honestly okay! Please don't stress about me.'

'Don't stress,' interrupted her father. 'You were just kidnapped by a bunch of bikies, left in the bush and then to top matters off you were in a fire. Of course, we are going to stress and worry about you.' Lara's dad Frank sat down next to his daughter on the couch, patting her knee affectionately.

'Anyway lovely, it's just good to see you at last,' Lara's mum said, putting her hand on her other knee. Lara felt so content having her mother and father sitting on either side of her like warriors protecting a precious jewel. She couldn't wait to introduce them to her new friends and the little community of River Bend.

It had been four days since Lara had been discharged from the hospital and it felt like the whole town had rallied around her. She thought she had put on a year's worth of weight with all the hot meals, slices and cakes people kept dropping off at her door. At this rate, she would roll into school next week instead of walk. Des had dropped off a whole lot of beautiful handmade cards from her grade, all telling her how much they missed their favourite teacher.

Her mum got up and started to fuss around the kitchen, wiping already clean counter tops and picking up some of the cards that were displayed on the bench. Each time she put one down Lara heard her mutter, 'beautiful words,' or she would let out an audible, 'ahhh.' 'Lara there are some lovely cards here. You certainly seem to have made some caring friends in town and, oh those little kids of yours really missed and care about you.'

'Mum I can't wait for you to meet my new friends. Marg has invited us to her place for dinner tomorrow night if that's okay with you guys. She's invited half the town to come and meet you both, as well.'

'That would be lovely, we can't wait to meet them all. If they're anything like that lovely policeman of yours and the owner of the Riverdale Arms, then I'd say we will have a great night.' Florence started going through the fridge getting out the cold meats and salad she had brought up from Melbourne for their lunch. 'Now tell me all about Curtis, he seems so different from Josh.'

'Agww, bloody Josh! I can't believe he had the gall to come to this town after everything he did to you during the lockdown. I flaming wish I had been there when he was at the hospital. I'd give him a piece of my mind to be sure.' A red tint crawled up Frank's neck to his cheeks as he spoke.

'Calm down Frank, remember your ticker and what the doctor said,' interrupted a worried Florence, patting her husband's arm.

'What do you mean Mum, what's wrong with dad's heart?'

'We didn't want to worry you love, what with you being so far away and with everything that's happened, but your father had a bit of a nasty turn and is now on heart medication for it. Don't stress love, it was caught in time and the medicine is working, but he's been told by experts to take it slowly.'

'Honestly love, those galahs don't know a thing. I'm fine,' said Frank, digging into his very healthy salad and ham roll.

Lara couldn't believe that her father had been sick and she didn't know about it. 'Mum why didn't you tell me?' she questioned, raising her eyebrows for emphasis.

'We just didn't want to worry you love and honestly it was caught in time, I am fine, just a few lifestyle changes to make, that's all,' interrupted her father, giving her mum the side eye.

'You've already retired, what life changes? Is it diet, less stress? Oh no, and now I've gone and caused you all this worry.'

'See love, that is why we didn't want to tell you. We knew you would worry,' sighed her dad.

'We were going to tell you but then this happened so of course it went on the back burner until we knew our girl was okay.'

'Honestly Mum, Dad, you don't have to worry about me; I think I've made a real home here in River Bend, and apart from the stupid Olsen brothers, everyone is lovely and supportive.'

'This is probably a good time to bring up the next chapter of our lives, don't you think Frank?'

'What now?' moaned Lara, looking intently at her mum and then turning to face her father. 'Come on out with it.' She had noticed that her father looked like he had lost weight, though not in an unhealthy way. He also had a nice tan as if he had been outdoors more, maybe walking or gardening.

'We've decided to join the grey nomads and see a bit of the country. What do you think?'

'That is the best news, I'm so happy for you both. Now tell me, where are you off to first?'

Marg opened the door on the first ring and warmly welcomed in the little party of Lara, Curtis, Janie, Paddy, Florence, and Frank. They came armed with gifts and food. Florence had helped Lara make a decadent chocolate cake dripping with cream and cherries for dessert, and Janie had brought along one of her most popular Asian salads. The boys were lugging a six pack of beer and two bottles of wine. They followed Marg out the back to the barbeque where Smithy was already flipping sausages and poking at T-Bone steaks. Lara introduced them to Frank and Florence and the younger boys took over the tongs, chatting about the great win River Bend Eagles junior footy club had over the Talbot Lions. Little Missy lay at Marg's feet in a patch of late-afternoon sunshine, content as Marg occasionally reached down to scratch behind her ears and let her know she was a part of the group.

'What a terrible state of affairs for our poor Lara. I'm telling you Florence the whole town was gobsmacked by the scandal of those Olsen brothers. You couldn't trust them as far as you could throw them,' sighed Shirl, patting Lara warmly on the arm and turning back to the table saying, 'Safe as houses now though, and finally dating our Curtis.'

'Even blind Freddy could tell those two were meant to be together,' nodded Pearl, smiling warmly at Lara and Curtis

'And I think our Janie and Paddy will be the next cabs off the rank.' Shirl winked and broke into a huge smile, looking over to the barbeque where Paddy, Janie, and Frank were talking. Someone must have said something funny as Janie put back her head and released her bigger-than-life laugh. Paddy was staring at her with adoration and Lara really hoped that they could make a go of it by somehow managing their busy work schedules. Lara looked at Curtis who had got up from the table and was heading over to the barbeque. She smiled at the warm feeling that enveloped her whole body as she watched him walk. He was looking particularly handsome in his tight blue jeans and crew neck jumper. He was so very different from Josh that Lara shook her head in wonder at staying with him for so long, especially with the abuse she suffered. A few nights ago, while she and Curtis were lying in her bed, she'd told him everything that had happened to her during the lockdown. She feared that he would judge her as weak, but he just enfolded her in his giant arms and rocked her as she cried, saying that even though he had been raised in violence himself, he could not believe that Josh had been so cruel to her. Lara had done a lot of in depth thinking and research over the past few days and realised that she had to move on and build her confidence and self-worth back up if she was going to rise from being a victim to being a survivor. She had even made an appointment with a psychologist in Talbot to finally be rid of Josh for good. Curtis was the perfect life partner for her, he gave her nothing but respect, love, and he deeply understood her mixed emotions about living with abuse. As she looked on at her friends it made her heart soar to see Curtis and Janie living a full and enriching life. Curtis looked over and saw her staring and gave her a friendly wave and smile, putting his fingers to his lips and blowing her a kiss.

Yes, she was one very lucky girl.

Lara's Research

You couldn't trust them as far as you could throw them: cannot be trusted at all.

Safe as houses: solid, strong foundation, safe.

Blind Freddy can see: love is obvious to everyone.

Next cab off the rank: next in line.

37

Chapter Thirty-seven

'You're back,' said a very happy Tom, when he walked into the classroom on Monday morning.

'Miss is back, you're back,' repeated Bill, with a huge grin on his face. This was his first official day at school with Lara.

Marg came up behind the boys and gave Lara a big kiss on the cheek. 'It's so good to see you back, Lara. How are you feeling after a week of rest?'

'I am so much better thanks to all my wonderful friends plying me with healthy food. Mum and Dad just loved it here as well. Thanks for having them over for dinner, Dad couldn't stop raving about your amazing hospitality,' she laughed, rubbing her tummy as if she were full. 'Des tells me you are going to be working temporarily with Bill in my room until we can organise a Learning Support Officer. I have some wonderful programs on phonics and number sense for you to look at and get your feedback as you worked with Bill all last week. Shall we get together after school?' Lara asked, opening up the door and being greeted and hugged by all her little students.

They had a great day together but by the end Lara realised it was going to take a while to get her body back to where it was before she was kidnapped. When she got together with Marg, Lara showed her some ideas she'd formulated for Bill. There were some great reading apps on the iPad that she thought he would like as well.

Marg opened up her computer and showed Lara a course that she had found online. 'I've had a bit of a development in getting a new LSO. Tiffany is really keen to work now that her girls are both at school and she's basically on her own in their new home all day. This online TAFE course looks perfect for her. What do you think?'

'That's such a brilliant idea. Tiffany would be amazing and it could give her a career now that her girls are both at school,' Lara replied, taking a sip from her water bottle.

'How are you feeling love? You look a bit pale, let's get you home so that you can have a rest before dinner.' Marg noticed how pale and tired Lara looked after her first day back at school.

'Thanks Marg, there is so much to do in this job. I am definitely not complaining but there's an overwhelming amount of admin to get done.' She closed up her laptop and put it into her backpack to work on at home.

'That's why I've been to Des to get this LSO thing organised as soon as possible. Oh, and there has been another development in the job department. You know how old Mr. Barry wanted to retire but couldn't find anyone to take over his bus run? Sam Wilson has applied for the job which means no more gallivanting across the countryside for him, he'll be here to look after his boys when they come home from school every day,' said a very happy Marg.

'That's fantastic news Marg. Everything is finally falling into place for the Wilsons. Goldie will be so happy. You know he really believed in Sam's innocence but had to follow through because of that sneak Barrington.'

'Goldie?' said Marg, pushing her eyebrows together.

'Oh yes,' laughed Lara. 'That's my nickname for Curtis.'

'I love it, you know Dave used to call me his little Dot,' she said wistfully.

'Little Dot,' asked Lara with her head to the side in thought.

'My real name is Dorothea but everyone at home called me Marg because I had an Aunty Dorothea and it became confusing. So, Dave, who knew my real name, called me 'little Dot. Lara are you okay you have gone positively white? Here take your water bottle sweetheart. I knew you came back too soon.' Marg handed Lara her water bottle from the desk giving it to a shaky and pale Lara.

Lara slid her hand across her face trying to compose herself. A few nights ago, Curtis had confided in her about Sam Wilson's search for his birth mother, Dorothea. What should she do! Just blurt it all out or talk to Goldie and see what he thinks before she passes on this huge life changing news to Marg.

'Darling what's wrong you are scaring me?' Marg was at a complete loss as to why Lara was reacting so dramatically and thought it was all to do with her recent kidnapping and ordeal.

'Marg can you please ring Curtis for me and ask him to come here? I really need to speak to him.'

'Of course, sweetheart, stay here and I'll ring him for you.'

Curtis arrived twenty minutes later and came into her classroom concerned that she was having a relapse after everything she had been through. He knelt down beside her chair and took her hands in his.

'What's wrong Lara?' he inquired, showing concern in his eyes.

'Marg, this actually concerns you.' Lara turned towards a confused Marg.

'What do you mean Lara? I don't understand.'

'Curtis, Dave used to call Marg 'little Dot' because her real name is Dorothea,' she said, staring intently into his eyes waiting to see his reaction.

'Shit! Marg please, you need to sit down. I have something really important to tell you.' he said, raking his hand over the stubble that had grown since his shave this morning. 'Sam Wilson came to River Bend looking for his birth mother. He only knew that she lived in River Bend and her name was Dorothea Maxwell.'

Marg took a deep breath and held her hand up to her mouth as if trying to hold in an escaped gasp. 'Oh my God Curtis I'm Sam's birth mother,' she cried out, as tears welled up in her eyes. Lara reached over and took the older lady's hand gently.

'He went to the council chambers but there was no record of a Dorathea Maxwell ever living in River Bend so he gave up looking, but decided to raise his family here anyway,' Lara explained, stroking Marg's hand with her thumb trying to get some warmth back into them.

'Can you take me to them Curtis? I need to see him and my grandchildren.' Marg stood up slowly reaching over and giving Lara a hug full of love. 'Thank you my girl you've made me very, very happy.' Tears of joy and love ran down Marg's face as she finally realised that after all these years she was going to be reunited with the baby she was forced to give up. This time however, she would be seeing Sam as a son and not a suspected criminal.

Curtis's ute pulled up out the front of Sam Wilson's cottage and the little party of three got out. The cottage looked very different from that first day when Lara had wandered in and discovered little Bill home alone. They had started clearing out the derelict garden and it looked like Sam had put in some summer plants. Two new flowering pots now adorned the still sagging veranda and the front window shutters were open in a welcoming way. Curtis had phoned Sam beforehand to tell him what they had discovered, he felt it would be too much of a shock to just turn up unannounced and throw a birth mother on Sam and his two boys.

Suddenly the front door banged open and Bill came running down the front steps yelling, 'Nana, Nana,' with his little arms outstretched ready to dive headfirst into Marg's arms. Behind him, Sam and Tom came out of the house a little bit more reserved, but still with shy smiles on their faces.

'Oh my little darling,' Marg said to Bill, kneeling down and hugging him to her with tears of joy streaming down her face.

'Don't cry Nana. I'm happy not sad.'

'I know my darling, these are tears of joy and happiness not sadness.'

Curtis and Lara stood at the back, watching the family reunion in awe. Sam came over and gave his mother a quick, shy hug. From the look of pure joy on Marg's face Lara knew in her heart that everything was going to turn out beautifully for the little family. Tom reached up and took Marg's hand in his. 'Come on Nana I want to show you our new veggie patch.'

Everyone walked around to the side of the house where they had started to make a new garden. As the boys showed Curtis and Lara the huge array of seedlings they had just planted, Marg and Sam spoke on the veranda together holding hands in the late afternoon sunshine.

38

Chapter Thirty-eight

As Lara stood on her balcony waiting for Curtis to finish work, she looked around the main street of River Bend. She couldn't believe it had nearly been a year since that fateful day she had run into the roo. So much had happened in a year. She had made best friends with many of the town's folk, started a wonderful job that she loved, become part of a community, and best of all, fallen head over heels in love with the local policeman. She also thought back to being locked in the back of the semi, bound and shaking for her life, and had to admit that it hadn't all been a bed of roses. There was the fire and the death of the farmer, who so easily could have been her had she made the decision to run instead of bunker down in the stream. The Olsen brothers and Barrington came into her thoughts and she physically shook herself to get them out of her mind. Yes, it had certainly been a full year.

One of her best friends Marg had finally found peace and met the baby she was forced to give up for adoption. They were such a happy part of the River Bend community now. Marg was like a different person. She doted over her grandchildren and was making a real connection with Sam; she had such a skip in her step. The little family were often seen going for ice-cream sundaes at the Cozy, Cup & Wares, little Bill always holding his Nana's hand. She had removed the double bed from her spare room and set it up with bunks and dinosaur themed bedspreads. She was like a completely different person. There was no sign of the sadness that followed her around after her beloved Dave had passed away. Her only regret, she had confided in Lara, was that Dave never had the joy of meeting her son and grandsons.

For Lara, the best thing was being with Curtis. Every time she thought of him a small hot flame went down her body, starting at her cheeks and ending up at her toes. Yes, just the thought of him made every nerve in her body spark. She hardly ever thought about Josh anymore and she certainly didn't ever compare the two of them. After all there was no comparison. Goldie was gentle, kind, loving and considerate whereas Josh...well she was not going to dwell on Josh's faults. He had done the one good thing by her and that was get her back safely into Curtis's arms.

The orange flowering gum stood out spectacularly against the blue of the summer sky. The pesky indian mynas were starting up their war cries looking around the street for food, probably a stray lizard to gobble up. Lara could see a tiny blue wren jumping in and out of one of the pot plants outside the CWA hall, it was probably scratching around for some tasty worms or thrips.

From over the road, she saw one of the Early twins bringing in the open sign from the IGA, leaning it against her hip for support. What the Early's brought to the town's community feel was amazing, they were such an integral part of River Bend. They seemed to be behind every raffle and CWA function, raising much-needed money for the school and community sports. Even after knowing them for nearly a year, she still wasn't confident in saying one of their names out loud. She laughed to herself. They had become like mother figures to her and were especially proud of the fact that Curtis and she were an item, as they believed they had it sussed on that very first day when she had met them all.

'Those two are a match made in heaven,' they would say to anyone that would listen.

She turned away from the scene in front of her and went into her apartment to check on the lamb in the oven. Curtis would be here soon, her heart sang at the thought of him. *Her Goldie,* she smiled to herself as she closed the oven door and finished preparing the evening meal.

www.ingramcontent.com/pod-product-compliance
Lightning Source LLC
Chambersburg PA
CBHW061212210726

48294CB00006B/1822